STRANDED

DOUGLAS WENTWORTH

STRANDED

The vacuum of space allowed Evelyn's hair to float freely, framing her face in spun gold. Her eyebrows and lips, animated just minutes ago with a strange amalgam of fear, wonder and curiosity, held a hint of surprise. The pale blue eyes, which had witnessed twelve years of life's experiences, were closed; the long, blonde lashes stilled.

If not for the golf-ball sized hole in Evelyn's forehead, she might be asleep.

It was this hole that intrigued Sandra Hapgood. She noticed that the inner brain matter had swollen, the result of its moisture boiling away. If Evelyn's eyes or mouth had been open upon her body's ejection from the ship, they would have swelled also. But Evelyn's death had been peaceful, and Sandra was content that she had killed her quickly.

The deck beneath Sandra's feet trembled slightly and, with her eyes still gazing at Evelyn's corpse, she instinctively began to swipe her hand across the window's sensor pad. But she abruptly stopped and rested her palm on the thick glass. Evelyn's hand was touching the other side, a mere four inches away; her fingernails soundlessly scraping the glass as the ship's main thruster engines began their forward thrust.

Sandra, her face a taciturn mask, slowly peeled her hand from the glass and swiped the window's sensor. Upper and lower solar shields noiselessly glided towards one another, steel eyelids slowly obliterating Sandra's view.

And, as the shields winked out its sole remaining emanation of light, the starship, *Prometheus,* gained momentum; cutting through the black velvet of space while plowing indiscriminately through the fifty-two human corpses that surrounded it.

SECOND EDITION, FEBRUARY 2014

ISBN: 0983420734
ISBN-13: 9780983420736
Library of Congress Control Number: 2014903370
Frank D'Angeli Publishing, Wakefield, MA

*I would be remiss if I did not acknowledge that
my passion for writing, and my writing style,
has been greatly influenced by the adventure
stories of Ian Fleming and his successors.*

I hope I have done them justice.

*I must thank David Hogan
and Andrew Bell, without whom
The STRANDED universe would not exist.*

To my loving wife, Jennifer

*Though we inhabited the same house
as I penned STRANDED,
I wasn't really 'there',
I was traveling through the cosmos,
chronicling the trials and tribulations
of six intrepid astronauts...*

It's good to be back.

STRANDED

"The future enters into us long before it happens."

– Rainer Maria Rilke

TABLE OF CONTENTS

PART I

THE BEGINNING OF THE END

1.
THE SEED IS PLANTED

"**D**o you know what you're doing?"

Before replying, Sandra looked up and across the kitchen table at her twelve-year-old twin sister, who was eating a big bowl of spaghetti. Eating was the wrong word; she was playing with it, twirling strands of the pasta around her fork in a way that would make Crick and Watson proud, for she formed a reasonable facsimile of a double helix. After admiring her work, she opened her mouth wide and swallowed the forkful. A stray, inch-long strand wormed its way out of the corner of her mouth, adding a pale yellow comma to her mocking smile.

"You're gross!" Sandra snarled. She abruptly turned back to the task at hand. Spread before her was a bowl of red delicious apples, canisters of sugar and flour, and a Pyrex pie plate. Sandra grabbed an apple, and in one swift motion, cored it with her mother's antique Kitchen-Aid utensil. She casually dropped it in a bowl to her right and reached for another. "And yes, I know what I'm doing."

1

"Sure you do." Her sister jerked on her pigtails and, like an old-fashioned lamp having its cord yanked to light its incandescent bulb, her tongue darted out.

"I hope you bite that off someday."

Sandra put the corer down on the family kitchen table.

Family. When a father just gets up and walks out one day, are the people left behind still a 'family'? Is that the right term? Or is it 'broken home'? Well, I guess it's better than being an orphan, thought Sandra. She turned back to the bowl of apples but her thoughts were still focused on that fateful day, four years ago.

Her father had abandoned the household when she was eight years old. One minute she was doing homework and the next thing she knew, her father came into the room and told her that he had to go somewhere; that he might not be back because he and mommy were always fighting. He said that wasn't good for her (I'm glad he was putting my interests first, Sandra thought sarcastically). And then, when she asked who would do the things with her they had always shared, like bicycling, soccer, and skating (her mother had an aversion to sports), he turned to leave and said, "You're on your own."

She remembered her eyes stinging as if she had been slapped in the face.

Are there four other words in the English language that can have such diametrically opposed meanings depending on their use? When the student pilot has successfully completed his training and it's time for the first solo, those words instill a sense of pride and accomplishment. But if that same pilot has instrument problems during that solo at ten thousand feet, those same four words mean nothing but abandonment and hopelessness.

The chair across from Sandra squeaked. And, like a dog trainer snapping its fingers to break the bored dog's obsession with licking its tail, Sandra's memories of that event slithered back into a dark corner of her mind and she looked up at her sister.

With childlike curiosity she studied the human mirror that sat opposite her. She contemplated the wavy, dark black hair that was so much like her mother's. She didn't like the splattering of freckles that covered her cheeks and nose like sprinkles on an ice-cream cone, but her mother promised her they would lighten with age. Of course, when she reached her teens, she could wear makeup.

And what about the eyes? Well, Sandra hoped that her big brown eyes didn't have the light of mischief dancing in them, as her sister's did right now. It made her untrustworthy for some reason, even a bit scary.

The doorbell started ringing; a harsh, buzzing sound that rattled Sandra's brain. She shot her hands up to her ears.

'Rrrrrr-Rrrrrr'

Why won't someone answer it?

'Rrrrrr-Rrrrrr'

Why won't it stop?

Her sister said matter-of-factly, "You're supposed to go now and save humanity...but are you sure you know-"

Even through her covered ears, Sandra heard her sister's words clearly. "I know what I'm doing!" she screamed back.

'Rrrrrr-Rrrrrr'

Sandra sat bolt upright in bed. The dream of her younger self dissipated like the ink of night at the break of dawn.

Now what the hell? Oh no.

The emergency lighting system was bathing the small, utilitarian room in a blood red pall. Sandra dove out of bed, zipped on her jumpsuit, and ran towards the door. She was halfway out when she turned back and quickly swept the room, her still dilated eyes wide with terror and anticipation. After taking the mental snapshot of the room she would never visit again, in a building that would crumble within the hour, on a planet that would soon cease to exist, she slammed the door behind her. Her diminishing footsteps echoed down the corridor in double time; a fitting coda to a fitful night.

Sandra exited the building and, as her deployment orders dictated, stood by the NASA CREW ASSEMBLY sign. The early morning Florida sun cast warm fingers on her cheek. How beautiful that sun was. White threads of clouds criss-crossed the sky in a checkerboard pattern, setting the stage for the gods of good and evil to play their penultimate game of chess. Would humankind win or lose? Flourish or vanish?

Captain Kalin Bennish stepped up next to her. He inserted an unlit cigar between his teeth, then placed his hands on his hips. His right hand reassured him the Beretta 92 was in its holster. He turned to address Sandra, his piercing blue eyes practically jumping out from the bronzed, worn leather face.

"Lieutenant, this will be our finest hour."

"What's happened, Captain?"

The doors behind them burst open and the other four crewmembers stumbled onto the waiting area.

Chief Mechanic Daniel 'Mac' MacNamara adjusted his tattered 'Red Sox 2004 American League Champions' cap. "They've done it, eh Captain?"

"Wait until we're on the transport," said Bennish. Like a conductor's baton, his cigar moved up and down in time with each word. "Come on. Let's load 'em up. Keep order, people. Hapgood, Minami, MacNamara, Rottweiler, Van Lank, let's go. Let's go!"

Sandra stepped onto the van-like transport, walked towards the rear, then slid into the last seat on the right and watched the others follow.

Commander Mineko Minami walked down the aisle with her head down and hands crossed at her waist. She looks like she just took Communion, thought Sandra. But her church mouse persona betrayed the crack pilot that she was, and Sandra was grateful that she'd be at the helm of the *Prometheus*.

Mineko shot Sandra a smile as she slid into the seat across the aisle.

Mac was next. He sauntered down the aisle, twisting his broad shoulders to avoid hitting the overhead storage bins. "Last call for the Escape Earth Express," boomed Mac. "Stragglers will be incinerated!"

"Grow up for once," chided Mineko.

Sandra smiled in spite of herself. Mac was like the proboscis of a mosquito, always getting under one's skin with his instigating comments and ill-timed remarks.

"Ladies!" Mac ignored Mineko's reprimand, tipped his cap, then folded his six-foot, four-inch frame into his seat.

Next on the transport was Power Specialist Eric Rottweiler. Eric avoided all eye contact as he headed for his seat, stole a brief look at the others, then grunted before he sat down. Though Rottweiler was in his early thirties like the rest of the crew, Mac had described his disposition as 'an old man with perpetually abscessed teeth', making Rottweiler one of those few people whose obvious nickname, Rott, match his personal temperament.

Sandra begrudgingly acknowledged him with an imperceptible nod. She then looked at the man stepping onto the transport and felt a warming in her heart, just as she had every day for the past year, from their first introduction at the *Project Prometheus* inception meeting.

Planet Assessment Specialist Ryan Van Lank smiled at each crewmember in turn. He shot a sly wink at Sandra as his disheveled dirty-blonde hair splayed in front of his twinkling eyes. The deep dimples on his cheeks and chin, gained a bit more shadow.

Van Lank stopped for a second before sitting down.

"Good luck, everybody."

The seated crewmembers responded in kind.

Sandra was pleased that the others liked Van Lank. It reaffirmed her belief in him, confirmed that her instincts were correct in having turned her heart over to him.

And what are the others thinking of me, Lieutenant and Chief Scientific Officer Sandra Hapgood? Graduate of Harvard Medical School followed by residencies at Carnegie Mellon and Johns Hopkins. A few years at the Air Force Genetic Medical Recovery Labs and then Lady Luck struck.

Happenstance put Sandra at the right place at the right time, for she had stood on the shoulders of giants.

She studied and modified her professors' experiments, then worked day and night until the prayed-for 'Eureka' moment. First, the successful lab trials, then the publishing of papers and the peer review process. And finally, the awarding of U.S. Patent Number 17459-28479: Digitizing Genetic Code and Basic Core Memories via Gray Matter Extraction.

Sandra was the first person named to the then secret *Project Prometheus* a little over a year ago. And now it seemed like just yesterday when the Chairman addressed them all with his 'We are going to save humanity...' welcoming speech.

The thud of the transport's door slamming shut brought the crew to attention. Captain Bennish waved his hand over a sensor on the dashboard. The maglev track became electrified. The transport, repelled by the magnetism beneath it, levitated, and then was propelled forward. They would be boarding the *Prometheus* in five minutes time.

Bennish pulled the cigar from his mouth, spit a speck of tobacco leaf on the transport's floor, and addressed the crew.

"At 04:00 hours cease-fire negotiations broke down. Within minutes a few small countries, figuring they had nothing to lose, let off a few of their nukes. As predicted, all neighboring countries retaliated. Europe is on the brink of destruction, Asia is next, and we are already tracking nukes coming at us over the Atlantic."

Rott spat out a single epithet.

Sandra's mouth went dry. She gathered some saliva.

"How long before..."

"About an hour. Now, we knew this was going to happen...just not today. Hell, our mission was based on it happening. So, the fueling has been stopped..."

Bennish held up a hand to ward off comments.

"...but we have enough for the mission. Now..." Bennish paused and looked each crewmember in the eye. "Now, we're going to do the job we were trained to do. We'll board, get systems operational, and prepare for liftoff. The gates will be opened and Hapgood will be stranding civilians up to the last possible minute."

Sandra's trigger finger twitched involuntarily. She remembered reading that Billy the Kid's finger used to twitch when he was sleeping, due to either the memory of those he killed or the anticipation of those to come. Or both.

How many had she killed, had she stranded, in the last month? How many had she stranded altogether? Let's see. About two hundred mice, two hundred pigs, a hundred dogs, twenty five terminally ill patients (should those count?) and five thousand perfectly healthy men, women, and children. Oh well, they'd thank her for it later.

The first twenty or so were tough. She hadn't perfected her aim and there were some that lived for a few moments. Tremendous suffering for the subject and humiliation for Sandra, for she had designed the brain-core extraction process. But with practice came perfection and soon she could terminate subjects before they even knew what hit them. But she couldn't take credit for all of the deaths, three thousand of them were done by others; she had only supervised.

Sandra gazed out the window and scanned the sprawling grounds of NASA; a concrete prairie poured into place on Florida's Atlantic coast. Just fifteen years ago she had made her first visit here. She and a group of friends had skipped school to see the last original Space Shuttle liftoff. Sandra looked to her left at the old Shuttle launch pad. Oh what a day that had been! The incredible roar of the engines had sent shock waves through her body that must've jarred something loose, triggering some deep, hibernating seed to sprout, take root, and reach for the sun, for she made a vow, right then, to explore the heavens someday. And now here she was, preparing for her seventh, and arguably her last, spaceflight.

A crease formed in Sandra's brow. Whatever happened to those classmates? Where in the world were they? Sandra bowed her head and prayed that their impending death today would be as quick and painless as possible.

Sandra looked up and contemplated the design of *Prometheus*. Thirteen hundred feet of polished ceramisteel, the strongest, most heat resistant ceramic-metal alloy in the world. The sleek, bullet shaped fuselage glistened in the morning sun. Long, lazy streams of condensation flowed down its sides, joining at its base like rivers to an ocean to form a translucent white pillow, which ebbed and flowed around the rocket's four fins.

Prometheus resembled those iconic rocket ships in old science fiction movies and Sandra was ecstatic over it. Heck, she half expected to see an astronaut step out wearing a Michelin Man-like spacesuit and a big glass sphere on its head! But the computers had spit out its design based on the needs of the mission and it coincidentally matched the old-fashioned hand drawings of those early space pioneers. Guess they were onto something even back then.

A half-mile behind the ship, wrapping around the launch area like a miniature Great Wall of China, was the hurricane fencing that had been erected two weeks ago. Thousands of people had gathered behind it during the past few days, hoping to gain entrance to the ship. The fencing was designed to funnel civilians to the gantry, like cattle to a slaughterhouse (how appropriate, thought Sandra). Once on the gantry, they would have to navigate the endless zig-zagging escalator. The prize at the top was the *Prometheus'* civilian entrance, where Captain Bennish would allow ten at a time to enter the Strand Extraction Lab, where Sandra would be waiting for them.

But today, something about the crowd was different. The fence was undulating like a sheet on a clothesline in heavy winds. Sandra realized that it was caused by the civilians fighting, kicking and clawing in a futile attempt to get to the front of the line. They had heard the news regarding the cease-fire and assumed, correctly, that the ship's launch was imminent.

The crowd numbered about seven thousand. Sandra would be lucky to process a few hundred of them before liftoff, if that. The 45,000,000 pounds of thrust that the *Prometheus* would produce on liftoff would quickly incinerate the rest of them.

The NASA engineers predicted a force of that magnitude, six times stronger than a Saturn V rocket, would destroy all structures in a half-mile radius. But the engineers didn't care. They knew that if *Prometheus* had to launch, NASA was doomed anyway.

The jerk of the transport coming to a halt pulled Sandra out of her introverted musings. Bennish was on his feet and out the door practically before it opened.

"Let's go, people. Let's go!"

The crew exited the transport's door and stepped immediately into the steel, cage-like elevator. Bennish engaged its motor before Hapgood's left foot had barely cleared the doors.

As they were lifted towards the ship's entrance, one hundred stories above in the nosecone, Sandra surveyed the area, willing herself to store forever these final mental photographs of Earth's wonders. Granted, they could view holographic photos and movies once they were all re-instantiated, or brought back to life, in eighty years time, but they would pale in comparison to this: the aqua blue sky; the peaceful, rippling blue-black water; the circular, fan-like leaves of the Dwarf-Palmetto; and the Florida Gama Grass, whose long green blades provided spots of color along the edges of the concrete launch pads. She would never see this sight or these images again. A shiver shot up her spine like a lightning bolt.

The elevator slowed to a stop, the rear exit door opened, and as Sandra turned to follow her crewmembers into the ship she thought what a strange day it had been. And to think it all started with that disturbing dream of her being a child, making an apple pie while her twin sister ate spaghetti. Why, she had never baked pastry in her thirty-year life! And as for the twin sister, well, that just made a strange dream even stranger, for Sandra was an only child.

2.
HADES ON EARTH

The roar of two jet fighters zooming by NASA's launch control building nearly shook the teeth out of Marlon Richemond's head as he stood, binoculars in hand, studying the *Prometheus*.

"Jesus Christ! Did you see that?"

Darren Callahan looked up from his monitor. "That's great. As if we don't have enough problems."

A split second later, the BOOM-BOOM-BOOM of surface-to-air mortar fire echoed off the surrounding buildings. The unmanned sentries, woken from their sleeping state, were firing skyward but, like drunken skeet shooters, couldn't hit the fast moving targets.

"Turn the machine-gun sentries on, continuous fire mode. Maybe we'll get lucky and keep those jets away from *Prometheus*."

Marlon flipped a switch. Outside the windows, thousands of bullets cut through the air skyward like an infinite swarm of angry hornets. Marlon sat down at his console and studied the screen. "The crew's been on board for forty minutes, ready to launch in T minus thirty."

"It's going to be tight." Darren consulted his screen. "Looks like the first nuke will hit Miami in about twenty minutes, then one with our name on it about ten minutes after that."

"At least it will stop the strafing." Marlon's cracking voice betrayed the humor in his remark.

"Out of the frying pan…" Darren let the comeback hang in the air. "But at least we'll see the *Prometheus* off. They've processed about forty of the civilians so far. That means they're leaving Earth with five thousand chosen by lottery, and however many they can do today." Darren spun in his chair to face Marlon. "That'll ensure genetic diversity when they make it."

"You mean 'if' they make it."

"They'll be all right. Top-notch crew. Bennish is hard so he'll follow through. We'll see the ship off safely then stand at the windows and watch nuclear fusion right before our eyes." Darren winked at Marlon. "That'll be one science experiment I won't be able to skip by playing hooky."

Marlon smiled meekly. He appreciated Darren's attitude. They were the only two technicians remaining in the entire NASA complex and Marlon was grateful Darren had stayed behind with him. When the lottery for slots on the *Prometheus* was held, both men had declined to enter. Neither of them was married nor had any next of kin. The idea of being in stasis, digitized and stored in a database for eighty years, didn't appeal to either of them.

On top of that, they knew they could serve the future of humankind much better here, in this room, than they could by being stored in some database onboard the ship. Yes, their jobs would be over, terminated in the most permanent way possible, but what a grand exit: the saving of humanity!

Marlon looked up at the row of video monitors that lined the wall like tiles of a mosaic. One monitor displayed the sea of people that were pushing and shoving through the gates. Another kept track of the *Prometheus'* gantry, which was covered in a moving sea of color; civilians that were trying to gain access. Marlon was reminded of a twig he had once stuck into an anthill. Within minutes, an angry black, writhing mass had covered the twig, forming one large living organism. This had repulsed Marlon, and to quell it, or perhaps to assure himself that his position in the food chain was secure, he pulled the twig out and flung it in a lake.

Well, that twig, which was now that gantry, was going to be flung into the ocean, by two forces stronger than his hand, yet forces forged by the hand of man. First, a vessel filled with explosive plasma gas would soon try to break the shackles of gravity and bring God's creation to another world where it would, hopefully, flourish again. The second force would be a weapon of ultimate destruction that would ignite one mile above them.

Marlon wondered which would impress God most, man's ability to destroy His world or the ingenuity man employed to escape it?

As if in answer to his question, one of the blank monitors came to life. The picture kept freezing and pixelating into blocky images and the audio dropped in and out. Marlon remembered how it had been years ago, when all broadcasts were analog as opposed to today's digital. Back then, if your TV couldn't latch onto a signal, the screen would be filled with 'snow', a constantly shifting black and white houndstooth pattern. But with digital, it was either picture or no picture. In this case, he wished it were no picture, for the man whose image appeared on the screen disgusted him.

The Chrysander (Christian name: Charles Chaconas) was born in Kuala Lumpur on May 14, 1990, the same day that it celebrated its one hundred years of local authority. His father, who owned a Greek shipping company, had moved the family to this capital of Malaysia in order to expand his base of operations to Port Klang on the western shore.

The young Chaconas excelled in school and had a voracious appetite for reading all things pertaining to religion and philosophy. While other children were out playing or swimming, he could always be found in his family's living area, laying down on his mat (his family lived like natives; using removable mats as bedding material to eliminate the need for bedrooms), absorbed in an obscure book he had found in his local library.

Charles was fascinated by the power that the great religious leaders in history held over their followers and soon he was engaging, and angering, the local priests, imams, and monks (Malaysia is a multi-confessional society that celebrates the major festival days of Christians, Hindus, Muslims and Buddhists) in philosophical debates; his main point being that since all religions had such glaring differences, they must all be wrong, and only their commonalities had a chance of being right.

By the time Charles was twenty, he had a following of subjects that had become disenfranchised with their own religion. Using every social network, podcast, and webcast service available, he soon amassed a global following. By his thirtieth birthday, the name Charles Chaconas had been systematically 'scrubbed' from all digital records and 'The Chrysander' was a household name.

When the resource depleted, polluted planet Earth became a hotbed of anxiety and mistrust between the countries that 'had' and the ones that didn't, it became clear that things would spiral into the ultimate 'war to end all wars'.

Rumors circulated that the United States had funneled huge sums of money into what other countries perceived to be a far-fetched plan to digitize, or 'strand' (nicknamed after the DNA strands that were sampled by the process) a diverse group of citizens. These strands, or genome maps of the individuals, would be stored in a database then sent off to a life-supporting planet some eighty Earth years away.

There, the digitized citizens would be re-instantiated by a process that would 'rebuild' them using water, amino acids, trace minerals and elements. Then the inhabitants of this new community would utilize the cryopreserved plant seeds, insect larvae, and animal embryos to resume the cultivation of crops and the breeding of animals. Until food could be grown locally, the 20,000 tons of irradiated and frozen food stored on board would have to do.

Leaders of some countries thought the idea so far fetched they called it science fiction, but their jaws literally dropped once the U.S. started building *Prometheus* and their informers and spies located in the U.S. confirmed its mission.

But The Chrysander had knowledge of *Project Prometheus* from the get go, for he had followers in all walks of life. And, like a splinter naturally working its way up through the skin, his subjects would 'pay forward' any information they were privy to that might affect their fellow man. Once *Prometheus* was common knowledge around the world, The Chrysander tapped into foreign anger and protestations and became the face of the anti- *Prometheus* movement. But unlike others that wanted to stop the project due to jealousy or competitiveness with the U.S., The Chrysander had a genuine concern:

If humans had ruined the planet Earth, what right did they have to travel to a distant planet and ruin that too?

And now, in Earth's final moments, The Chrysander was the last person that Darren and Marlon would hear preaching.

They both looked up at the monitor, where The Chrysander, passionate and red-faced, was pounding his pulpit. "If you bring forth that which is within you, it will save you. If you do not, it will destroy you."

Marlon shook his head. "Still preaching to the choir."

"I don't sing," spat Darren.

The Chrysander was now appealing to the camera. The storm had passed. The piercing blue eyes, so fiery a minute ago, were now relaxed. The skin, which earlier resembled third-degree sunburn, was now pink, as it continued its transformation back to translucent white. He passed his hand through his hair, comb-like, in a futile attempt to tame his salt and pepper mane. Sweat stains showed through his cream T-Shirt which, combined with black jeans, comprised the only outfit that he ever wore in public.

He continued calmly. "All our technology and machines and efforts have only sealed our fate by increasing the potency of evil that we are. The evidence is irrefutable, the sentence…unavoidable."

"I wish he'd…Oh my God!" The color drained from Darren's face as he looked back at his monitor. "I'm tracking a nuke heading towards us from Tampa Bay! An undersea launch!"

Darren slammed his hand down on his microphone switch. "Captain Bennish! Launch immediately. Repeat. Launch immediately. Missile ETA in five minutes!"

Marlon and Darren immediately flipped the switches that released control of the ship. Darren engaged his microphone once more.

"*Prometheus* stranding process postponed. Will be resumed post-launch. Hand over and transfer of control to *Prometheus* on my mark…now!" Darren paused for a second then resumed. "The wishes of the good human race are with you. Control out. End of entry. Darren Callahan, National Aeronautics and Space Administration, 05:40 hours, June 6, 2026."

Darren turned to Marlon and forced a meek smile. "You never know, someone might listen to it someday."

Marlon was silent. What could he possibly say now that would mean anything? He reached over and flipped a switch. As if on cue, both men stood up and walked like automatons to the window.

It was a surreal scene. Jet fighters buzzing the sky, anti-aircraft mortars and tracers streaking after the fighters, and thousands of bullets following the mortars as if in a game of 'Tag'. And, about a mile away, the four main thruster engines of *Prometheus* ignited in perfect unison like synchronized swimmers in an old Esther Williams movie.

Both men stared impotently as the civilians on the gantry and mooring platform scrambled for cover, but there was nowhere to go, nowhere to hide from the six thousand degree Celsius heat and flame that would soon engulf them. They watched the launch pad's concrete turn to liquid chalk and the nearby buildings fall like houses of cards.

Hades on Earth, thought Marlon.

Behind Marlon and Darren, on the monitor that would soon be darkened forever, The Chrysander continued. "And yet there are cowards among us who believe the psychopathic humankind should spread. We chose our fate; now our actions ensure it. Let it go and let it be. This is the hour of destiny. The end of destiny..."

The broadcast abruptly ended. But Marlon and Darren didn't notice; they were concentrating on the *Prometheus* as it cleared the top of its mooring platform just as a jet fighter threaded its way through NASA's defenses. They watched in horror as an anti-aircraft mortar clipped the fighter's wing and sent it hurtling into the melted mooring platform. The resulting explosion and fireball engulfed the base of the ship. Shards of debris sliced into one fin and thruster. But the ship continued skyward.

"That was close," squeaked out Marlon after practically swallowing his tongue. He turned from the window, visibly shaken, and sat at his monitor.

"May God protect them," prayed Darren.

"He's not protecting us," countered Marlon. "Look."

Darren turned toward his monitor. His face drooped and twisted as if he suffered a major stroke. On the screen, seven other nuclear launches from the submarine off Tampa Bay were projected on a course for NASA, along with hundreds of other trajectory lines traversing every country and ocean.

Thoroughly defeated, Darren and Marlon didn't move; they just stared out the window. They followed *Prometheus'* path until she was just a dot in the sky. Then, in the distance, a single nuclear missile appeared. They watched it arc serenely, almost majestically, over the horizon and, as it reached its zenith directly above them, someone turned all the lights in the world on at once. Their eyeballs melted and their bodies, along with every building and life form within a twenty-mile radius, vaporized within a second.

3.
THE END OF THE WORLD

When Bennish and the crew had stepped into the entry area of *Prometheus*, they immediately scrambled to their assigned areas, like roaches reacting to a flipped light switch.

Mineko headed to the cockpit, and with a trained eye, scanned all the data that was streaming in from the ship. Usually, if any system: autopilot, hydraulics, coolant, fuel, etc. generated a 'system check' error, the flight would be delayed, but not this time. They had to launch no matter what and they'd only have one shot at it. And though the flight path was preprogrammed, Mineko would be able to disengage the autopilot within seconds if her considerable skills were needed. That is, if Bennish allowed it.

In a normal NASA flight, a Commander like Mineko would be in charge of it and all other crewmembers. But *Project Prometheus* was under military command, so Bennish had been deemed leader of the mission. Mineko was to follow his orders. She wasn't used to that but she believed in the chain of command and she knew one bad link would weaken it, so Mineko promised herself she'd swallow her pride and do what was right for the greater good.

Oh well, thought Mineko, we'll all be in stasis in a few days and I won't have to follow his orders again until the ship finds an inhabitable planet in about eighty years or so. We'll be re-instantiated three days before we land and, once we do, I won't be under Bennish's command any more.

Mineko turned in her seat and glanced through the bulkhead door. Bennish, in his usual rough and gruff manner, was directing civilians, one small group at a time, toward the Strand Extraction Lab. She wondered how many Sandra—

The intercom system screamed to life.

"Captain Bennish! Launch immediately. Repeat. Launch immediately. Missile ETA in five minutes!"

Mineko quickly hit the master override switch, which would put the ship in launch mode. She turned to see Bennish slam his hand on the wall-mounted intercom and, with spittle flying from his mouth, scream into it. "*Prometheus* crew, scramble. Repeat. Scramble. Prepare for launch!"

The civilians on the gantry, having heard the announcement and Bennish's reaction, surged forward, pushing and screaming, desperate to gain entry to the ship.

"Back off!" demanded Bennish as he slammed another switch on the wall. The entrance door began to slide close, but as it sensed the bodies, arms and legs of the now desperate civilians still clawing their way onto the ship, it paused and reversed itself.

"Minami!" screamed Bennish. "Override the door!"

Mineko, noticing that some civilians were still only halfway onto the ship, placed her finger lightly on the door control switch, waiting for them to clear harms way.

"Minami! Override that door now! Goddammit!"

Mineko flipped the switch then turned and grimaced as the sounds of crunching bone and blood curdling screams echoed in the entranceway.

Bennish jumped quickly back from the door, so that the severed extremities would not land on his feet. The last civilian that slipped onto the ship, appalled at Bennish's disregard for his companions, stared into Bennish's eyes.

"For the love of..."

Bennish punched the man in the mouth. Then, angered that the man's now loosened teeth left indentations in his knuckles, he slugged him with his other hand. The man fell to the ground like a sack of pig iron.

Bennish turned to the other twelve men, women and children that were still in the entranceway, waiting to enter the Strand Extraction Lab. They stared at him fearfully, like a class of pupils being introduced to the headmaster.

"Get down and grab something. We're going to launch!"

Bennish scurried to the cockpit and strapped himself into the copilot seat. He turned to Mineko. "Light her up, Minami."

"Yes, sir." Mineko flipped the steel guard, which prevents buttons and switches from being thrown accidentally, up from the launch panel and revealed the four switches that would ignite the main thrusters. As she consulted a status screen, Bennish, annoyed at what he thought was delay on Mineko's part, slapped her hand away and flipped the switches in one movement.

"Captain. That wasn't necessary," protested Mineko weakly.

Bennish turned in his chair and leaned his face directly into Mineko's. For a second, she thought she was looking into the wild eyes of a madman.

"Don't you ever, ever, question one of my orders. Got that, Minami?"

Mineko had to turn her head. The stench of Bennish's breath was like fire in a sealed room; it stole the oxygen. To cover what might be considered by Bennish to be a breach of manners, Mineko quickly looked down, as if in a pose of remorse, and through gritted teeth said, "Yes, sir."

And as this test of wills was playing out, *Prometheus* was slowly lifting from the launch pad, a skyscraper sitting on a lobby of fire, lifting it skywards.

* * *

Major Mark Dwyer swiped his finger up, then down, then up again on the surface of his touchpad. He was confirming the space station's manifest and shut down procedures. For a second, he felt bad for Bennish. Boy, that mean son-of-a-bitch must've rushed like hell to get *Prometheus* ready once he, Major Dwyer, notified him that the space station's monitors had spotted nukes heading across the Atlantic.

Dwyer could imagine Bennish trying to keep his cool, while that temper of his boiled like magma beneath the Earth's crust. And, like that magma, Bennish's anger would erupt once it found a weak point, or a crewmember Bennish pegged as weak-willed. Dwyer prayed that whoever that person was, he or she would find a way to pay Bennish back in kind.

"Major Dwyer, sir? The *Prometheus* will be docking in five minutes. We are ready for evacuation. Are there any other duties I should attend to?"

Dwyer swallowed hard and turned to Mission Specialist Larissa Ketanka. He reflexively wiped his hands on his pants (they always became moist with sweat whenever he laid eyes on Larissa) and wished he had popped that mint in his mouth that he had contemplated earlier. He hoped that the sound of his heart, which always beat in double time when the Russian beauty entered his surroundings, was not being heard outside of his middle-aged, yet fit, body.

"Yes, Ms Ketanka, I would like to make love to you; slow, passionate love. Something I've wanted to do since you took up residence here a year ago."

Major Dwyer didn't say it, but he thought it.

"Thank you, but no, Ms Ketanka. We are all set. Please just take your station and report the progress of *Prometheus*."

"Yes, sir." Larissa's golden, shoulder length hair (cut to military regulations) moved forward and back from her beautiful elfin face as she nodded. She slid her lithe five-foot, five-inch body into her seat and stared at her monitor. Her brow furrowed immediately.

"Major Dwyer, sir? The *Prometheus* is on course to dock with us, but her speed is increasing, not decreasing."

"That can't be…" Dwyer quickly moved to a position behind Larissa and leant over her, his head practically resting on her shoulder. Even in this time of stress, his mind subconsciously registered Larissa's natural scent (perfumes and colognes are banned from spaceflights), and a tingle shot down his spine to his groin. His conscious mind was only concerned with the computer graphic that showed the trajectory of a very large icon named 'PROMETHEUS' intersecting and then passing through the tiny icon named 'SPACE STATION'.

"What the hell is that stupid bast-" Dwyer grabbed the microphone. "Space Station to *Prometheus*, Space station to *Prometheus*. Come in. Over."

Silence. Just a bit of interstellar static.

"Space Station to *Prometheus*! Come in. Over!" Dwyer's voice wavered a bit.

"Major Dwyer, sir. Impact in one minute." Larissa turned her head slightly to look at Dwyer. His jaw was set hard. His eyes were large and Larissa could see the gears spinning inside that brilliant pilot brain of his, weighing options and judging odds.

Dwyer's mind was working furiously. All engines had been shut down. He had no way to vent any gas, oxygen, or anything that would cause a force strong enough to nudge the space station out of its orbit. He was in a position of hopelessness.

When he was a child, he and his sister had walked down to the corner store to buy blue-vanilla Popsicles. They were strolling along innocently with their beloved dog, a collie-shepherd mix named Dusti. As they walked home, a neighbor's dog charged the fence they were passing and scared the hell out of them.

Dusti instinctively ran into the street (there were no leash laws in that small Texas town) to avoid the perceived threat. When she reached the far sidewalk she circled back to make a run at the offending dog.

Dwyer's heart still hurt when he remembered seeing, as clearly as if it were yesterday, the truck barreling down the street. He saw his dog barking and running full speed, her concentration solely on the dog that had harassed her masters. Dwyer couldn't stop it. A collision was inevitable. He could've closed his eyes or turned his head, but he didn't. He did remember yelling out, "Dusti!"

The truck slammed on its brakes but it was too late. The bumper caught Dusti broadside and she was rolled under it.

Even today, some thirty-five years later, he could not explain what went through his head at the time. It was a combination of 'I'm going to see something I love die right now' and 'how am I going to deal with what I'm about to see?'.

Dwyer looked at Larissa. Her eyes were pleading, hoping that he was going to say something brilliant, save them from the inevitable. But there was nothing. No tricks from a magic hat, no heroics that they would be able to joke about for the next fifty years at spaceflight reunions. No, they would not be holding court with a group of old-timers, former astronauts that were hearing the story again for the upteenth time, who would begin to laugh when he'd say, "Larissa, remember that time when that idiot Bennish almost rammed us?"

Dwyer swallowed hard. No. They were the dog in the road, the slow hanging curveball, the nail sticking up from the floorboard. They were about to be whacked. And Dwyer cursed the heavens that the only thing that came to him, the only words he could offer one of the most gorgeous creatures that God had ever created, was this:

"Get down and cover your head."

If Larissa was disappointed in Dwyer, she didn't let it show. She pushed back her chair and deftly dove under the table. She scrambled into a sitting position.

Dwyer, feeling more impotent than he had ever felt in his life, numbly climbed under the table opposite her. He looked at her and smiled meekly.

"Mark, come under here with me." Larissa patted the floor next to her.

Mark? Mark! Larissa had never called him by his first name. Dwyer scrambled out from his cover and crawled next to Larissa. They were squeezed shoulder to shoulder. Larissa looked into his eyes and placed her hand on his cheek. A thousand fireworks went off in Dwyer's head.

"Mark. Please, I must tell you. My feelings, I mean. I love you."

You can take me now, God, Mark thought, for I have heard the greatest words ever stated to me in my life.

Dwyer gently took Larissa's face in his hands. "You, Larissa, are the most beautiful girl I've ever known, and I love-"

Mark could've sworn he was able to read the letters 'P-R-O-M' on the fuselage of the ship that tore through the space station. He remembered holding Larissa's face in his hands and then the floor opened up and his world shattered into a million pieces. And now he realized his eyes were shut and he was slowly exhaling. Training. Yes, it was his training that made him close his eyes and exhale his breath after the collision.

When he was in astronaut training school years ago, he remembered reading about the accident in 1965 at the

Johnson Space Center Vacuum Chamber. An astronaut's suit had developed a leak and he was exposed for about fifteen seconds to the same conditions as the vacuum of space.

Scientists had learned that holding your breath would likely damage your lungs, and regardless of the myths, Dwyer knew he wouldn't immediately explode, or have his blood boil, or instantly freeze into that blue Popsicle he loved as a kid. He knew he'd probably live for a minute or two before he blacked out from lack of oxygen.

But, as luck would have it, he had been speaking when the ship hit and his lungs were depleted. He had maybe fifteen seconds left before his next futile gasp for air. Of course, it wouldn't find any in the vacuum of space and his body would then reflexively go into spasms, jerking like a hung man at the end of a botched execution. It would then be only a matter of minutes before his gaping mouth would set in the rictus of death.

But before that happened, he had something to do. He'd always been disappointed that man couldn't leave their space vehicles without space suits. He yearned to see space with the naked eye, not through multiple layers of heat shielding, sun blocking, and optically distorting glass. No, he had always wanted to see it without a fishbowl on his head and now he had the chance!

Dwyer opened his eyes. The stars were shining like diamonds. The spinning, rotating splinters of the space station reflected the reds, orange and yellows from the *Prometheus'* exhaust, which was now about ten miles away. Of Larissa, there was no sign. Why had his hands let her go? Oh, that's why, thought Dwyer when he looked down. His right forearm had been severed just below his elbow, and his right leg was gone also.

Dwyer was about to look around for Larissa but then his vision blurred. He realized the moisture from the surface of his eyes was boiling away so he closed them. Hell, he was out of breath anyway. He would think of a few good thoughts then he'd take that futile attempt at a next breath and start that journey to the light that we all begin the moment we leave the womb.

He smiled as he remembered that Dusti survived her accident and escaped with only a fractured hip. She lived happily for five more years. And best of all, the best memory of his entire life had happened only seconds ago. Larissa Ketanka said she loved him.

4.
STRANDED

"We'll be docking with the space station in two minutes, sir. *Prometheus* to automatically decelerate in thirty seconds," stated Mineko as she studied the display before her.

"Auto-pilot off. Take manual control, Minami." Bennish was guiding the last of the civilians through the Strand Extraction Lab doors.

"Sir?"

Bennish clenched his fists and looked sharply at Mineko. "Minami, what did I tell you about questioning orders? Shut that damn auto-pilot off!"

"Captain Bennish, sir. I programmed the auto-pilot myself. It will position us optimally and we'll dock with the station perfectly. I appreciate you trusting me to guide *Prometheus* under manual control but I'd prefer-"

Bennish walked over to Mineko, reached across her, brushing her breasts as he did so, and flipped the auto-pilot switch and the external communication channel off.

"Commander Minami," said Bennish through clenched teeth. "You are to keep up speed and not alter course."

Mineko looked at Bennish curiously. What is this guy doing? What is he talking about? Could there be any beneficial reason why he would order such a thing? Maybe there was and she wasn't seeing it. Mineko started to doubt her own judgment.

"Captain. May I ask the reasoning behind your order?"

"Commander Minami," Bennish used his most soothing voice. "As we've discussed, something clipped the number four main thruster on liftoff. Until MacNamara can do a visual inspection we cannot shut the engines, they may not start again."

"Sir, even if thruster four was totally disabled, it would have no effect on the other three."

"Commander, this is the most important mission of all time. Humankind is counting on you and I..."

"But sir, If we stay on course we'll destroy the station; we'll kill everyone on board. At least let me veer off course to avoid them!"

"We have to put the life of my five crewmembers, the strands of over five thousand people, people just like you and me, people that are going to contribute to the continuation of the human race, we have to put all of those lives above the ten people on that station. Neither of us can guarantee that if we veer off course, we'll be able to resume. Now, are you with us or against us?"

Mineko looked at her display. If she were going to dock with the station she would have to start the deceleration within ten seconds. But what if Bennish was right? What if docking with the station, or even altering course to miss it, put the mission in jeopardy? No. She couldn't risk it. She better do what Bennish ordered.

Mineko kept the ship steady, the speed constant.

"That's better, Commander," said Bennish as he stared out the cockpit windshield at the silver dot that was the space station. "I'd speed us up a bit. The faster we hit the station the less damage it will do to us. Physics, Minami, the law of physics."

Mineko pressed the accelerator lever forward. The silver dot in the cockpit window grew larger. If there had been a crosshair painted on the windshield the space station would be dead center to it.

As the number of miles before impact decreased, the number of tears in Mineko's eyes increased, so that by the time they hit the station she could see nothing.

"Well done, Commander, well done."

The lump in Mineko's throat made her gag. She had to consciously get her tongue to push her saliva to the back of her mouth and then order her throat muscles to swallow. Some saliva went down her windpipe and she started coughing and spitting.

Bennish patted her on the back, turned quickly on his heels, and exited the flight deck.

Probably going off to steal another crewmember's soul, surmised Mineko. And with that thought rattling around in her head, heart, and stomach, she reached for a barf bag.

* * *

"Hurry it up, Hapgood. All hands meeting in five minutes." Without waiting for an acknowledgement, Bennish, who was leaning into the Strand Extraction Lab, backed out and the door slid closed.

Sandra didn't feel like answering. There had been a five-minute meeting with the crew a half hour earlier, in which Bennish barked out orders, stressing the need to complete tasks that were neglected due to the sudden launch. That didn't leave much time for questions, and when Van Lank had queried why *Prometheus* did not pick up the space station crew, Bennish had launched into the same story he apparently had sold to Mineko.

Sandra could sense that none of the others had bought it and she could see the look of self-loathing on Mineko's face. Everyone must've been thinking the same thing; that Bennish was an ass for his blatant disregard for the station's doomed personnel, or, he lacked faith in the ship's ability. The former was beginning to become typical behavior while the latter would not be the best way for him to show confidence in their mission.

Granted, main thruster four had been hit by debris, but most of the diagnostics were still pretty darn near normal. And Bennish had ordered the ship to a full halt about a quarter hour after hitting the station, so why was it okay then and not earlier? Bennish said it was because they were far enough away from Earth's gravity. That's true, but still, something's just not right with that guy...

Once they had stopped, Sandra resumed the first half of her reason for being on the ship, the stranding of human beings (her second responsibility was to ensure the data integrity of the strands), and she headed back into the Strand Extraction Lab. And though the lab was the last room the civilians would see until they were re-instantiated in about eighty years time, it was Spartan in appearance; certainly not memorable.

About the size of a tractor-trailer, the lab was split into two parts. The entranceway was nothing but a simple holding area large enough for about ten people. There was a divider that separated the waiting subjects from the one being stranded. It was deemed best to keep the stranding of the subject out of the line of vision from the others; for it was a disturbing sight. Then, once the next subject was beckoned, the person would walk around the divider to meet Sandra, and their fate.

On the far side of the divider, the subject would enter something very familiar to anyone who'd ever visited a doctor's examination room. Familiarity would put the subject at ease. About fifteen feet square, the room had light tan walls dotted with a few non-descript paintings. A couple of flowering, potted cacti (they would need minimal care) dotted the room with spots of color.

Against one wall was a desk, upon which laid a slate glass keyboard. Its associated monitor was wall mounted behind it. Next to the desk was a doctor's stool and beside that one of the most advanced pieces of electronic equipment ever devised and constructed by the hand of man, the Strand Sampler, though you would never know this by the look of it.

The sampler was about the size of a small refrigerator, the type you might find in a dorm or hotel room, with a holster-shaped slot on its side. Inside of this slot rested the strand sampler gun, which was roughly the same size and shape as a hair dryer. Flowing out of the right hand side of the sampler's 'barrel', were individually wrapped, four-inch long plastic tubes, joined side to side. They entered the sampler gun sequentially like belted rounds of ammunition. The sampler's simplicity in design betrayed its complexity in function, as the entire future of humankind rested on its silicon, plastic and steel construction.

Jutting out from the wall next to the sampler was what looked like a bed or gurney. A faint line in the wall above, with the exact same dimensions, would reveal to an observant eye that the gurney would be able to fold up into the wall; like a sleeping berth in a train compartment.

This would all seem normal to a casual observer except for one thing: a Hispanic man's body was resting on the gurney and it had a hole the size of a golf ball dead center in its forehead.

Sandra pressed a button on the sampler and the gurney started to lift up and retract into the wall. Like the wheel of a steamship, as the gurney moved up, another appeared from the wall beneath it. The Hispanic man's body was deposited behind the wall and, within a few seconds, was ejected from the ship. Sandra reset the system and prepared to call the last subject.

5.
EVELYN

"**N**ext!"

Sandra, mentally and physically exhausted, sighed and rubbed her eyes. This was it, number fifty-two for the day. Then that's it! Well, not really. In a few days time, once the crew had finished their duties, they too would be stranded and put into stasis. Then Sandra would lay down, put the sampler on automatic, and trust that with no human to supervise, it would save and process her brain matter into a digitized genome map of herself in addition to ninety-nine percent of her memories and emotions.

Sandra squeezed the top of her nose between her thumb and forefinger then took a deep breath and turned to face the last subject: A twelve year old, blonde haired, blue eyed girl.

"Please step over here and look at that spot on the wall." Sandra pointed to a colored tile on the floor then to a flush mounted camera lens on the wall.

The girl approached then stood with the instep of her right foot resting on the calf of her left leg, like a flamingo might stand in a shallow pond. Like an obedient schoolgirl, she held her clasped hands at her waist. Yet, she didn't seem nervous. Her eyes were bright and she was smiling. This surprised Sandra, for she couldn't remember the last time she had seen a civilian smile.

Once the young girl was in position, there was a flash of light as the girl's photo was taken. Sandra glanced briefly at her monitor, which now displayed a picture of the girl.

"What's your name?" asked Sandra.

"Evelyn," the young girl said proudly. "Evelyn Himmel." Evelyn looked at Sandra with a quizzical eye. "What's yours?"

"Excuse me?" said a distant Sandra as she picked up the strand sampler gun. Her finger instinctively slid through the guard and centered itself on the trigger.

"What's your name?" repeated Evelyn.

"Hapgood."

Evelyn scrunched her nose. "Is that your first name?"

Sandra looked into Evelyn's eyes for the first time. "It's Sandra."

"Nice to meet you, Sandra Hapgood."

"You too. Now let's get you situated."

Sandra helped Evelyn lay down on the gurney, where she squirmed a bit trying to get comfortable.

"Try to relax now, Evelyn, and don't worry. The technology is sound, the equipment is foolproof."

"My daddy says it was technology that got us into this mess in the first place."

Sandra had been moving the sampler toward Evelyn's head but stopped. "And it will get us out of it. Now, let's get settled. I promise you won't feel a thing, and you won't feel anything in stasis either."

Evelyn sat up. "Are you sure?"

Sandra softened a bit. "Yes. You'll close your eyes now, and it will feel like only a couple of seconds before you wake up again."

Evelyn smiled and laid back down. "Okay Sandra, I believe you." Evelyn's smile vanished. "Am I the last one?"

"Yes, why?"

"Because I lost track of my parents. They had pushed me through the crowd, and some of those people were kind enough to keep pushing me forward but then I lost track of them. I was hoping they might have gotten ahead of me. Does 'Himmel' sound familiar? Are my parents stranded?"

"I'm sorry, Evelyn. I don't remember stranding them. I'm afraid you're on your own."

Now I've done it, thought Sandra, as she saw the stung look on Evelyn's face. The victim had become the perpetrator.

"Oh, I see. It's like that."

"No, not necessarily," Sandra stammered. "We processed a lot of people today, maybe I'm just forgetting." The lie tasted bitter on Sandra's tongue as she spit out the words.

"That's nice of you Sandra Hapgood." Evelyn's voice sounded defeated then quickly brightened. "Hey, will you take care of me, talk to me? You know, while I'm in stasis?"

"You want a running commentary of our progress? You won't be able to hear anything."

"Well, I think I just want to know that someone's out there, you know, watching over me."

Sandra stared at Evelyn for a few seconds. "I'll tell you what. We, the crew, are going to be stranded ourselves in a few days, so I'll be in stasis with you. But I promise that until then, I'll talk to you. Deal?"

"Deal!" Evelyn stuck her hand out and Sandra, after shifting the sampler to her left hand, shook Evelyn's. She then moved it back to her right.

"And now, Miss Himmel, it's time to say goodnight."

"Goodnight Miss Hapgood. You'll take good care of me, I know you will."

"Close your eyes now, Evelyn, you won't feel a thing."

Holding the sampler gun like an experienced marksman, Sandra placed its muzzle against the center of Evelyn's forehead. There was no need for Sandra to look up at her monitor, where computer generated crosshairs would guide her to the proper target. For Sandra could do this with her eyes closed, and she did close them for a moment as she pulled the trigger.

Evelyn's body shivered for a split second then stopped.

Sandra began to put the sampler back into its slot then stopped, thinking better of it. She held the sampler in front of her, pointed it towards the ceiling, and squeezed the trigger.

The four-inch long transparent tube jutted out from the sampler's barrel. The tube was filled with bone, skin and brain matter. To Sandra, it was a beautiful thing. Everything that Evelyn was, that Evelyn is, was contained in that tissue sample. The secret code, the incredible genetic recipe, which at one point only God knew, was now reversed engineered. And, thanks to Sandra's research, a series of chemical breakdown and reaction tests, coupled with the *Prometheus'* array of supercomputers, would break that recipe down to a series of 1's and 0's; the language of computers.

Satisfied, Sandra released the trigger. The tube slid back into the barrel, and Sandra placed the sampler into its slot.

Immediately, on the monitor, a series of G, T, A, and C's, raced across and down the screen. After about a minute, the letters stopped and the monitor displayed:

> DNA SEQUENCED
> SYNAPTIC MEMORY MAPPED
> SUBJECT'S NAME?

Sandra turned towards the microphone that jutted up from the strand sampler as if it was a King Cobra ready to strike. She enunciated clearly, "Evelyn Himmel." Sandra looked up at the monitor's readout.

> PROCESS DATA?

Sandra pressed the button and the wall opened once more to accept the exiting gurney. The monitor prompted:

> EJECT SUBJECT?

And, for the fifty-second and last time that day, Sandra pressed the button.

The intercom crackled to life.

"Hapgood. What the hell is taking you so long? Ready Room, now!"

Sandra watched the gurney come to rest flush with the wall. She yelled out, "Coming!" then headed out the door of the lab. But instead of turning left, which would lead her to the Ready Room, she turned right, towards a large oval outline in the ship's hull.

Sandra swiped her hand over a sensor pad and the upper and lower panels that comprised the oval silently separated, one up, one down. Sandra was now staring out of a window constructed of four-inch thick Lexan, and the last body ejected from the ship, Evelyn's body, was floating alongside, just outside the window. The other fifty-one bodies were floating all around the ship, like planets to a sun.

Sandra had stranded dozens of children, some outgoing and friendly, others quiet and docile. Sandra had wondered if some were even worth stranding. The New World would need strong-willed people, like the adventurers and settlers of the frontiers in man's past. She had never liked the idea of a lottery system; she believed that the subjects should've been handpicked. So as Sandra stood staring at Evelyn, at the hole she had just drilled in the young girl's forehead, she felt relief that a child like Evelyn, someone that embodied a special human spirit, would be resurrected in the New World.

Sandra touched the glass opposite Evelyn's hand and made a silent promise. Though every strand was important to her, to the mission, she would check on Evelyn's every once in a while before she herself went into stasis. Just to make sure no corruption or any unforeseen database problems interfered with a successful re-instantiation of Evelyn version 2.0 in about eighty years time.

The shudder under Sandra's feet subconsciously registered that the ship was starting to move again. And with the promise of Evelyn's survival signed, sealed and delivered, Sandra swiped the window sensor and snuffed out her view.

* * *

"Where the hell have you been?"

Bennish was standing outside the Ready Room's doors, arms folded across his chest.

"The children took longer than I expected," replied Sandra.

"Those children were breathing our air and depleting our resources, goddammit!" Bennish now had his finger pointing at Sandra's chest, jabbing the air in unison to his words.

Screw you, thought Sandra. "My priority was to the strands, to create them from the civilians as accurately as possible. And that's what I did."

"Your priority is to my orders. That's what you do!" Bennish had taken a step forward and his finger was now only a few inches away from touching Sandra's breastbone.

Sandra could feel her blood beginning to boil. If that finger touches me, I'm breaking it off, she thought. "May I remind you, Captain, that the purpose of this mission is those strands?"

"My orders are the mission!"

Flecks of Bennish's spittle settled on Sandra's chin. She wanted to vomit. What had happened to the man overnight? Up until this morning, he never showed this dark side of his personality. Did the stress finally put too much of a load on the see-saw of balance in his mind? Or would he wake up tomorrow and be back to the Bennish of yesterday, last week, last year?

Sandra strode around Bennish with purpose and, as the Ready Room doors automatically slid open, she spun on her heels, looked Bennish straight in the eyes and said, "I know what I'm doing." And with military precision, she spun back around and entered the room.

6.
SIX LITTLE INDIANS

Every crewmember on the *Prometheus* was a veteran of space travel, but that didn't prepare them for the view of Earth that the room's window, which curved around one quarter of the ship's fuselage, afforded them as the steel shutters opened.

Once Sandra took a seat between Van Lank and Mineko, it was only a few seconds before Bennish entered. He glanced out the window as he took a position in front of the semi-circular shaped table that faced it.

"Looks like we got out in the nick of time."

The crewmembers didn't reply. They were staring at the scene before them. From their vantage point, the Earth looked as big as a blue and white baseball held at arms length. About ten times per second, flashes of light would appear on its surface.

"Looks like each country has fired every nuclear weapon in its arsenal," said Van Lank, trancelike.

"They did. 'Cause nuclear bombs are like potato chips," said Mac as he watched the others turn towards him quizzically. "You can't just launch only one," he explained. "Once you open up that bag of hurt, you're going to finish them."

Son-of-a-bitch, thought Sandra, that's true. We're witnessing a war without any winners, and both sides know it. So it's a matter of hurting the other guy as much as possible, by loosing off a collective twenty-two thousand nuclear warheads. Stupid bastards.

Sandra clenched her jaw as she watched the flashes of light continue. She was instantly reminded of something. Yes, that was it. Now what were they called? Disco ball? Mirror ball? No. Glitter ball. Yes, if it weren't for the cloud cover diffusing the lights, that's what it would look like. Earth had been reduced to one big gaudy ornament for the amusement of the universe.

"Do we have to watch this?" queried Mineko as she slowly swiped her hand over a sensor on the table.

The shutters began to close again.

"What do you mean 'have to'? We want to. Captain Bennish?" pleaded Mac.

Bennish casually turned and looked behind him. "Leave it."

Mineko stopped her hand in mid-swipe and the shutters stopped, leaving just enough exposed window to view the Earth.

"I can't believe it's really happening," said Van Lank.

"Well it is, and all that means is we have a job to do. So let's take the minute," commanded Bennish.

Take the minute. Sandra looked around as everyone bowed his or her head, then she lowered hers. During the past six months, each crewmember was required to see a psychologist weekly to prepare themselves for what looked like the inevitable; the mourning of their friends, family, pets, etc., if and when the unthinkable happened. They had to practice something called Pre-Event Grieving, in which they would learn to cope with a disaster that did not yet happen. This meant that they had to act is if everyone around them, except for the stranded subjects and their five crewmembers, were already dead. That way, if the unthinkable happened, the crew would take one minute to say their prayers then get on with the mission, which the psychologists hoped would be cathartic, as they would be working to save the human race.

Sandra hated this grief counseling. It made her look at the people she saw every day as if they were already dead, like walking zombies. She distanced herself from technicians that she usually loved to share precious moments of downtime with, because as she was talking to them, she couldn't enjoy the moment. Then again, thought Sandra, how do you think they felt? They knew they didn't have a ticket to the stars. They knew they would most likely die on Earth or live like scavengers in a barren, post-apocalyptic wasteland.

But the psychologists had explained to the crew that most humans are optimistic, and though they expected bad things would happen, they personally would somehow manage to survive it. Maybe their cities would be spared nuclear destruction, or perhaps the world's leaders would come to some last minute agreement and order the nukes to self-destruct in mid-flight.

In other words, said the psychologists, since those people (including themselves!) would be dead, and the subjects would be in stasis, only the crew would have to face an uncharted level of grief. And yet, they were supposed to mourn twelve billion souls in sixty seconds!

Sandra finished her moment of silence and looked up at Bennish. Apparently, he had spent the entire minute staring at his watch, as he was looking with intense concentration at it now. She could see his lips counting the seconds. Did Bennish ever grieve anything? Well, maybe once when his gun jammed or something.

When the minute was up, Bennish, like a pistol shot, stood straight up to attention.

"Status reports. Van Lank?"

"Planet assessment scanners are one hundred percent. I'll do a full planet sweep once we reach the celestial border."

"Good. Minami?"

Sandra looked to Mineko, whose appearance caused Sandra's heart to drop. The usually sparkling, almond, cats eyes, were now opaque. The straight, jet black, shoulder length hair was practically standing on end. The peaches and cream, silk-smooth skin was now pasty and clammy, drained of color from whatever morbid thoughts had occupied Mineko's head during that somber minute. The small, yet perfectly proportioned body seemed to have lost half its weight, as if the day's events had drained not only her soul but flesh and blood as well. Mineko was one of the most beautiful women Sandra had ever seen, but she seemed to have aged ten years in three hours.

"MacNamara and I are running diagnostics on main thruster four," answered Mineko slowly and methodically. "Its status screen was displaying a warning."

"Yeah, the 'check engine' light was on," said Mac humorously.

"Too bad we can't call AAA," retorted Van Lank.

The small touch of humor among the last six survivors of Earth was welcome.

"Rottweiler?" Bennish asked.

"Power sources are fluctuating. Since the ship is designed to use engine power to generate bankable electricity, thruster four's problem is going to affect the power cells; they won't get fully charged. We'll need to pick up power somewhere."

"Well," said Bennish sarcastically. "I'm glad you didn't take my suggestion last year that we use nuclear energy instead of your jury-rigged system. You may have killed the mission before we've even started it."

Rottweiler fumed. "I didn't damage the engine! And you know right damn well that nobody here, not you, not nobody, wanted to be in stasis for eighty years while an unmanned, untested nuclear reactor kept the night-light burning."

"Keep up the attitude, Rottweiler. You just keep it up." Bennish looked slyly, menacingly, at Rott.

"Look!" said Mineko pointing at the window.

There was a change in Earth's appearance. Thick, black clouds covered the entire surface. Thousands of orange flashbulbs broke through the surface. Earth was now a blackened cotton ball with a lit match inside of it.

"I read," Mac began, "that during World War II, Hitler had scientists working on the atom bomb. One of them told good ol' Adolph that there was a chance the bomb would ignite Earth's atmosphere and Hitler didn't want to be responsible for something like that."

Rott shook his head and grimaced. "So instead, he found other ways to kill seventy-eight million people."

"Well," said Mac gesturing towards Earth. "Those guys just turned Hitler into an amateur, they just wiped out twelve billion."

"But who's counting, right?" said Rott.

Mineko bowed her head in silent prayer. She quietly slipped her hand into her right pocket and slowly pulled out, just far enough to see, an old fashioned, 3" x 5" photograph. It had been in color once, but the dyes and inks had faded over time, and the corners of the Kodak film were dog-eared, but it was Mineko's most prized possession.

When Mineko and her parents had first moved to America, she had been upset that she had to leave her home, her neighborhood, her friends. Her parents sympathized, and they promised her that they were going to do something special once they landed in the United States.

Mineko remembered stepping off the Japan Airline plane at JKF International Airport, squeezing her mother's hand tighter and tighter, and being directed up the walkway towards the lounge area. She had only felt this nervous once before, when she was five years old. She had been in yochien (kindergarten), on stage but behind the curtain, waiting for her initial appearance in her first play. She had the rite-of-passage butterflies. Would the audience like me?

But the stage was now halfway around the world in a foreign land called New York, and she was walking into a hustling, bustling terminal of the most famous city in the world. Would the Americans like me?

Mineko's mother brought her into the ladies room and they were both mortified when they saw the rudimentary ceramic bowls that would never pass as toilets in Japan. Where was the washing system, the seat warmers, the deodorization system? This is a dirty place, thought Mineko, I refuse to sit on one of those. And then her mother pulled a protective sheet from the box on the wall and placed it on the black plastic toilet seat.

I see how Americans do things now. They use a piece of paper to cover their embarrassments. Mineko turned to her mother, "Can we go back home now?"

And her mother had laughed and pulled some summer clothing out of her carry-on and told Mineko they had one more plane to catch. And when the next flight landed and Mineko felt the heat through the plane's metal skin and heard the pilot announce that it was 5:35 p.m. and 83 degrees in Orlando she was confused. Orlando was in a place called Florida, nowhere near the northeast coast of the United States that she had studied in preparation for her trip.

But after they collected their luggage, and stepped into the limousine, the nice driver tipped his cap and asked her, "Is this your first trip to Disney World, little girl?"

And Mineko was ecstatic. Her parents had promised her a few days in Tokyo Disney 'when she was old enough to remember', and apparently, a few months after her seventh birthday, here on her first day in the United States, the time had come. And when she stood in front of Cinderella's Castle, dressed as a little princess, with a parent on both sides, and when the gentleman in the pink striped shirt, white pants and top-hat, took the picture, she knew she had arrived and it was real.

And that photo, that snapshot in time from one of her happiest moments on Earth, the Earth that was now a blackened ember in a spaceship window, always brought her a touch of joy. And right now, she needed as much joy as possible.

"MacNamara. Report."

Bennish's voice pulled Mineko out of her reverie. She looked up at him as she surreptitiously slid the photo back into her pocket. Though Bennish was addressing Mac, he was staring at her. And when he saw her arm moving, his brow furrowed.

"All of the ship's major functions; life support, gravity generators, hydraulics, etcetera, are running fine," said Mac. "The only concern, as we've mentioned, is thruster four. I'll link into its diagnostics and see what's going on with it."

Bennish turned to face Sandra.

"Well, well. We come to Chief Scientific Officer Sandra Hapgood: The star of the show. The one in charge of the strands, which as she just reminded me in the corridor, is the only reason we're here. The rest of us," Bennish waved his hand from one end of the table to the other, "are just supporting cast members. When they write the book someday, I wonder if we'll even be mentioned."

Sandra swallowed hard and glanced at the others. They were all looking at her quizzically. But she knew they were on her side; and that they were also wondering what the hell had gotten into Bennish.

"Well, sir, if you're inquiring as to the status of the strands, I was able to strand fifty-two civilians. They've been entered into our database with the other five thousand.

As soon as I leave here, I'll head to the Strand Data Room and begin my monitoring of the data."

Sandra looked hard at Bennish.

"If I may, Captain, I'd like to address the crew."

Bennish gave a mock bow. "Go ahead. Be my guest."

Sandra slowly looked at each crewmember in turn. "Everything on this ship, every system, every bolt, was designed, manufactured and implemented in a year. You should all be very proud. It was a Herculean effort. And even though we prioritized and hit every commitment date and everything's running more or less fine right now, I'd like to remind everyone that even if our quality control ensures that 99.99% of every part of this ship is perfect, that still leaves ten thousand defective parts".

Everyone around the room nodded their heads. A few chuckled.

"Now, maybe most of those parts are just some bolts on the agricultural equipment, or the excavation equipment, or something that we won't even need for another eighty years. But there's also the chance that it's one of the thrusters' regenerative power supplies, or some chip in the planet assessment computer, or a bad batch of capacitors in the strand database servers. But whatever it is, we have three days to make sure that everything is running as near to perfection as possible, because I, I mean we, owe it to those strands to bring them back as human someday."

Sandra took a deep breath then stood up.

"If you'll excuse me, I'm going to start examining data. Because I know I'm going to do everything I can," Sandra turned to the doors and as they opened she stepped out and looked back at the crew, "not to screw anything up."

Bennish yelled after her. "I didn't dismiss you, Hapgood."

Sandra, walking away, answered over her shoulder. "I've got a job to do, Captain."

The door shut and Bennish turned back to the crew. "What did I tell you? The prima donna. Look's like Elvis has left the building."

"I'm sure she's just anxious to get back to the strands, sir," Van Lank interjected. "As I'm sure we all are to get back to our duties. Three days are going to fly by."

Bennish rubbed his chin for a second. "Right," he said drawing the word out slowly. "Rottweiler, I'd like you to dispose of the severed body parts at the entranceway."

"Why me? It was you and Minami that did it."

If anyone had been privy to Bennish's mind just then, they might have run for cover. Through gritted teeth he said, "Yes. We did, didn't we?"

"Don't worry, Rott," said Mac, trying desperately to lighten the mood. "If you need a hand you can probably just pick one off the floor."

Mineko, who was sitting next to Mac, punched him in the arm with all her might.

7.
THE TRUE NATURE OF MAN

STRANDS INSTANTIATED:	5,052
CORRUPTED:	0
VIABLE:	5,052

Sandra read the words on the wall monitor and was relieved. She let out her breath in a long whistle, then leaned back in her high-backed, luxurious chair.

She'd have to thank MacNamara for that chair later during dinner for she was sure it was he that had authorized it. He knew that Sandra would be spending most of her time in this, the Strand Data Room, and he believed the more comfortable she was, the easier her job would be. Mac realized that once the crewmembers were re-instantiated, Sandra would be sitting in that chair and, like a conductor with musicians, would be orchestrating the re-instantiation of 5,052 other human beings. And that would take time, a lot of time.

Sandra's head was sinking back into the acoustically transparent pillow, which would not distort music emanating from the embedded speakers. A person could get lost in this chair, thought Sandra, for it practically enveloped her. She felt like a young child, sitting in a theater's upholstered seat, with her feet hardly touching the ground, while she looked up at the huge movie screen and ate popcorn.

Well, she didn't have any popcorn with her but the analogy was correct. The Strand Data Room was, by all definitions, huge. Forty feet long on each side with one wall comprised of a large, single monitor, which stretched from the floor to a ceiling some twenty feet high. This monitor displayed nothing but strand data, which was represented by 5,052 photos of all the stranded subjects. Each photo was outlined in green, which meant that the person's data was intact and free of any corruption or inconsistency that would render re-instantiation impossible.

For the next three days, Sandra would concern herself with this monitor only, as the ones on the side walls, which were now off, would be used later, in eighty years or so. There were a total of ten monitors and they would allow her to monitor the Recombinant Labs, the rooms where the subjects would be brought back to human form. Sandra looked forward to the use of those rooms more than anything else in the mission, for the greatest day of her life took place in the very first prototype of just such a room.

When Sandra created the first strand sampler, it was nothing but a hypodermic needle that could extract some material from a simple, eukaryotic organism (fungi, animals and plants are examples of species that are eukaryotes). But Sandra was able to take that material and ultimately convert it to a digital file, a tremendous breakthrough. But what good was it if the file could not be re-instantiated back to its original form? Sandra had only solved half the problem; she had a great parlor trick but no encore act.

Luckily, Sandra had some extremely intelligent young researchers assisting her; geniuses in their own right. They were able to devise a way to have strand data converted into an instruction set that would control a flow of water, proteins, and trace minerals into a beaker, where these elements would be bombarded by electrical and chemical reacting agents. It took two years of testing but on one bright, sunny Thursday morning, they were able to re-instantiate the penicillum fungi. Boy did they celebrate that night!

From there, the milestones progressed quickly. Once they were able to re-instantiate a mouse, and it remembered where it had hidden its food, they knew they had solved the last stumbling block, and they were testing the process on humans within a year. Sandra was extremely proud that, besides a few botched stranding attempts (the computer generated targeting system had a 'bug' in it!) every human came back within parameters (no physical defect that was not already present) and 99.99% of intelligence and emotional disposition unchanged in any way.

Sandra had dreams and visions that one day she would strand people and have the computers fix any errors in the genetic code; curing Down syndrome, cystic fibrosis, sickle-cell disease, etc., but the global tensions started rising and *Project Prometheus* took precedence over any and all research.

And now, here she was.

Sandra leaned forward in her chair. She looked up at the wall monitor as her fingers deftly touched the glass keyboard.

On the wall monitor, a photo of a twelve-year-old girl zoomed to enormous proportion while the other photos faded into the background. The photo displayed its own information regarding its strand viability. Its green border, and the text which stated '100% Integrity' signified all was well with Evelyn Himmel's strand data.

Sandra turned in her chair to face the Human History Computer, which was about the size of a paperback book. Its associated display screen rested beside it. Sandra swiped her finger across the computer's glass top. Glowing blue icons representing media playback controls appeared. Sandra engaged the 'record' button and spoke into a thin, gooseneck microphone. "Hi, Evelyn. You're safe and sound. I'll be heading to dinner soon. A few more days and I'll be in stasis with you. Good night now."

Sandra engaged the 'rewind' button, released it, and the computer's screen came to life, displaying a news anchor's commentary. The anchor was standing in front of the White House, speaking gravely into the camera. "Diplomatic relations have broken down…"

Sandra fast-forwarded a bit. Now it was a NASA official. "…technical hurdles have been cleared, and an emergency crew is being assembled. The war's escalation…"

Fast-forward again. A NASA conference. Sandra, along with the other crewmembers, was addressing an audience of technicians. "Approximately five thousand strands will keep our gene pool at the proper diversity level and ensure-"

The camera began to swing wildly, due to a commotion in the crowd. It finally settled on The Chrysander, who had somehow gained entrance to this secure room. Security guards grabbed his arms and dragged him back, kicking and screaming. "...our continued destruction, the endless repeat of our tragic history..."

Hapgood, disgusted, fast-forwarded. A file photo of Darren Callahan appeared as his audio entry played in the background. "The wishes of the good human race are with you. Control out. End of entry. Darren Callahan, National Aeronautics and Space Administration, 05:40 hours, June 6, 2026."

Sandra stopped the video. She recalled Darren and Marlon's dedication and devotion to the mission and took a second to honor them. She then hit the 'record' button and spoke into the microphone. "Chief Science Officer Sandra Hapgood resuming history. Status of mission: Five thousand and fifty-two viable strands. Premature take-off required a number of civilians to be left behind. Planet Earth subjected to total nuclear destruction. Survivors: none. Cause of event..."

Sandra paused, thought for a second, then continued. "Man's will. Or lack of it." And, with her nose curled as if she just smelled bad fish, Sandra turned the history computer off, exited her seat, and left the room.

* * *

"Extinction: It's what we do."

Rott was making his case. Perhaps their mission was misguided. Perhaps man had no right, no right at all, to find a pristine planet and populate it with humans, humans that carried the seed of hate, violence, racism, and a whole host of other shortcomings.

The crewmembers were sitting around a long table in the Galley, the scraps of their hermetically sealed, irradiated chicken and dumpling dinner piled before them. Just a few minutes ago, they were actually joking, laughing, but that mood had soured and now Rott's observation was going to poison the atmosphere even further.

Earlier, when Sandra had left the Strand Data Room and entered the Galley, she was happy to find Mac there alone, extracting a cup of peach flavored tea from the brewer.

"Mac, I have to tell you, that chair you ordered for me is heavenly."

Mac looked up and smiled, genuinely happy. "Want to know a little secret? If you lower the gravity in that room just a smidge, you'll be floating a tiny bit in the chair, not enough to notice, but just enough to take all pressure off your back and bottom."

"But Bennish locked down gravity settings in all areas. How can I change it?"

Mac walked over to the Environmental Control Pad, a small glass square on the wall next to the door. He touched the pad and was challenged for a security code. "I hacked into the system. Bennish uses his military serial number as his password for everything." Mac read off the digits as he entered them. "Two, six, three, five, two, seven, seven."

The pad's screen came alive, displaying the current temperature, time, and gravity setting, which were represented by a virtual slider bar. A virtual arrow rested on its midway point.

"The center point is Earth's gravity." Mac slid his finger across the glass pad and decreased the room's gravity setting. Mac and Sandra felt themselves lifting a couple of inches into the air. "In the gym, this works wonders for my weight lifting capabilities."

Mac slid the gravity slider back to the midpoint and they settled back into their original positions.

As if on cue, the doors opened and the rest of the crew, Mineko, Rott, Van Lank and Bennish, entered the room.

The mood was basically relaxed for the first time that day. The expectation of some hot food, cold drinks, and at least a little time to sit back and relax was welcomed. And, like most working men and women do when they share a meal, they discussed and rehashed the events of the day.

At one point, as they were finishing their dessert, MacNamara groaned and the others, concerned, turned to him.

"I'm not feeling well. Something's not right with my stomach."

Mac picked up his napkin with his left hand and started to wipe his forehead. That's when it happened.

The sternum area of Mac's white T-shirt bulged outwards for a second and then turned blood red. Mac groaned and grimaced.

The other five crewmembers immediately stood up, their chairs flying back and toppling to the floor. Bennish, who was sitting opposite Mac, had his Beretta out in a two handed grip, his sights trained on Mac's midsection.

Mac's shirt kept bulging rapidly, repeatedly, a little further each time, as if something was trying to burst through his chest. Then, as quickly as it started, it stopped.

Mac pulled his right hand out from under his T-shirt and threw the burst little ketchup packet onto the table. He laughed heartily while he wiped the ketchup off his right hand. "Man, you should've seen your faces!"

Mineko was the first to speak. "Mac, you asshole!"

Bennish, uncharacteristically, was chuckling at the practical joke, as was Van Lank. Rott smiled, though he seemed distant, as if his mind was focused on other things.

Once the crew had picked up their chairs and sat back down, Sandra, who had found the stunt amusing, spoke up. "When I first saw that movie, I thought that would be the scariest thing in the world; to be alone in a spaceship millions of miles from home and have something burst through my body like that."

"Yeah," said Mac, "that would put a kink in your responsibilities for the day."

"Well I don't think we have to worry about an alien being on board and ruining the mission," countered Van Lank.

"Wait a minute!" Mac stood up, spun his cap around his head, and started pacing back and forth; one hand behind his back and the other holding an imaginary pipe; all in all a reasonable impression of Sherlock Holmes. "Maybe it wouldn't be an alien. Remember, this ship is run by computers, and they've been known to ruin missions and kill off crewmembers."

Chuckles from the crew, and then Mac made a fatal mistake.

"Captain Bennish!" commanded Mac.

Sandra would remember later that for some reason, the second Mac addressed Bennish, she had a feeling of dread and doom, not for herself, but for Mac.

"Captain Bennish," repeated Mac, "Would you do us a favor and sing slowly, in a low voice, the words 'Daisy, Daisy, give me your answer do....'"

My God I can't believe he just did that, thought Sandra. In Stanley Kubrick's sci-fi masterpiece, *2001: A Space Odyssey*, the crew of the spaceship, *Discovery*, are essentially murdered by the ship's computer, HAL. The last remaining crewmember accesses HAL's memory modules, and as he removes the last one, HAL recites, in a low, distorted voice, the first words he ever learned, the lyrics to 'Daisy Bell'.

Sandra looked at Bennish's face, hoping he hadn't seen the movie, wouldn't make the connection that Mac was implying; that Bennish was a danger to the crew like HAL. But the daggers that sharpened in Bennish's eyes, and the sly menacing smile that formed on his lips, proved beyond a reasonable doubt that Bennish knew Mac was mocking him. And there was no way in hell that a man like Bennish would let that slide.

Dammit, thought Sandra. Why hadn't Mac quoted some obscure sci-fi movie; there were thousands of them! Why did he have to quote a classic, something that Bennish was bound to be familiar with? Sandra saw that Bennish was going to speak. She swallowed hard and listened.

"Well, I'm not much of a singer," said Bennish with mock humility. "But you know what I can do, MacNamara? I can play the bugle, and I never get tired of playing 'Taps'."

The sweat appeared instantly on Mac's forehead, yet he kept a smile plastered on his face and tried to speak, but his voice caught a dry spot and he produced nothing but a cough-like grunt.

Van Lank jumped in. "Let's hope that some of the people we have in stasis are very creative; so once we have our new community established, we'll be able to look forward to new movies, books, plays, paintings…" Van Lank's voice trailed off.

Bennish looked from Mac to Van Lank. Though his words were benign his voice had the malignancy of terror in it. "Yes," he said slowly, a faraway look in his eyes, "One can hope."

Mineko steered the conversation further from the collision course Mac had set. "It's so hard to believe that we have to start all over again. It took humankind thousands of years to create all of the beautiful buildings, sculptures, temples, churches…and now they're gone. It's like there was no point to it at all. And the sad thing is, everyone saw it coming and no one stopped it."

"Sadder than that are the nutjobs, like The Chrysander, that were praying for our destruction until the very end," said Sandra.

This brought a rise out of Rott. "He wasn't praying for it, he was accepting it. Extinction is the end result of everything we did. Think about it. We poisoned our world and wiped out thousands of species, even hunted some of them into extinction, even though we knew we were doing it! For God's sakes we even extincted ourselves! It should be man's motto, his epitaph." Rott held up his hands to signify a quote. "Extinction: It's what we do."

Rott let his words sink in. "And what you saw happen today to the late, great planet Earth, well, that was extinction to the nth degree."

"I'm no English major," said Mac. "But I don't think 'extinct' is even a verb."

This brought a smile from everyone but Rott, who still sat stewing in his seat.

"The Chrysander was only saying that we had no right to seed another planet and extinct that one too."

"Well now, Rott," challenged Bennish, "If you agree with The Chrysander, why are you here?"

"It's better than being on Earth."

"Oh, that's a nice attitude," said Mineko.

Rott was incredulous. "What are you talking about? It's a human attitude. All we ever did was compete against each other. Sports, business, politics, it's all the same thing. Deplete, exhaust, devour. Winners and losers. And what could be the only result? Annihilation, that's what. Game over."

Sandra thought for a second. "But everybody was annihilated."

"Yes, eventually. That's what I'm saying."

"Wait a minute, Rott. There were people on Earth that wanted to fix things. You had philanthropists..."

Rott jumped out of his seat. A nerve had been touched. "Philanthropists! Are you kidding me? The biggest so-called philanthropist of our time made his money through crooked business dealings. He was convicted of it, for God's sake. And what happened to him? What punishment did he receive? Nothing. He quit his business and gave a bit of blood money to charity, scrubbed his history from the internet, and now has people like you calling him a philanthropist," Rott spit out the next sentence. "Don't talk to me about those assholes."

"But you can't deny that their money helped people in need," argued Mineko.

"I can't?" Rott took a deep breath, exhaled, then sat back down. He spoke with controlled anger. "Okay, let's take our famous philanthropist. He donates money to children's charities. They provide vaccines to poverty stricken children in Third World and war torn countries. A good thing, agreed?"

Everyone nodded his or her head.

"Okay. Well this philanthropist had also invested huge sums of money into companies that manufactured munitions: guns, bombs, and missiles. You know what I mean. So his charities would inject a vaccine in a kid's arm, and one of his bombs would blow that same arm off. And what do those kids become? The ones with the vaccines became a write-off, the ones with their arms and legs blown off became a blip on a chart, another uptick on a profit sheet."

Silence for a second as Rott's tale sunk in.

"Rott, not everyone is like that," said Sandra. "Look at us. Every person on this ship, every strand, is proof that man can act, will act altruistically. We're not saving ourselves here, we're saving the human race."

"Sandra," said Rott calmly. "There were other astronauts, other techs and scientists that wanted to be on this ship and we were chosen. That means, in a way, that we competed to get on this ship."

"So?"

"So even in our best impulses, we extinct each other."

Rottweiler stood up and made a sweeping gesture; encompassing everyone in the room. "Winners..." Rott then pointed out the window at the ember of Earth. "...and losers."

Rott turned and walked out the doors.

Bennish stared after him. His eyes fixed like black marbles. Rott and MacNamara were treading on thin ice, and it was melting rapidly. Bennish decided he was going to see that things got hotter very quickly.

PART 2

THE POINT OF NO RETURN

8.
CORRUPTION

Sandra swallowed hard. She blinked her eyes a few times for she couldn't believe what she was seeing. But the monitor didn't lie, it only displayed the status of the data the computers sent to it, and right now it was displaying heart-wrenching, gut-twisting information:

STRANDS INSTANTIATED:	5,052
CORRUPTED:	3
VIABLE:	5,049

She knew it the minute she walked into the Strand Data Room and saw the wall monitor opposite. A few of the five thousand plus photos were outlined in red instead of green. Sandra practically flew across the room and took her seat. Her fingers slid furiously across the keyboard, bringing the photos of the affected subjects to the forefront. None of them were Evelyn, thank God. She then checked and double-checked the afflicted subjects' strand viability. But there was no doubt; their strand data had become corrupted.

Sandra turned to the intercom. "Captain. I need to see you in the data room."

And Captain Bennish had answered affirmatively and now here she sat, waiting to tell the man in charge of their mission, the man she now thought was ill-qualified to lead a Boy Scout troop, that she, a Nobel Prize winning scientist, had somehow screwed up. How could things go from being so good to being so bad in five minutes time?

When Sandra had left the Galley just a short time ago, Van Lank had caught up with her. He was going to stop by his quarters on the way to the Planet Assessment Room, where he wanted to spend an hour or so before bedtime, checking his planet sweeping computers. There wouldn't be much for him to do except watch a monitor so he figured he'd bring a good book with him. Sandra stated that she would walk with him on the way to fulfilling her own duties.

It was with some amusement that Sandra scanned the contents of Van Lank's quarters once they arrived and he opened the door.

Two walls were covered with shelves that groaned under the weight of overflowing books. On the back wall, above the bed, were two of Van Lank's watercolors, which were unfamiliar to Sandra. She walked across the room and studied them.

One was a painting of a beautiful shoreline. Lush, green vegetation framed beautiful white sand, which was being lapped by deep, azure colored water. The sun shone brightly in the periwinkle blue sky. It was beautiful. It was paradise.

"Hawaii?" queried Sandra.

"Nope," said Van Lank with a smile.

"Bermuda?"

"No, and I'm not going to tell you. You'll have to keep on guessing. Now, want to try to guess what the other picture is?"

Sandra trained her sites on the other painting. It portrayed an ornate entrance hall to some elaborate, unseen room. One wall of the hall was covered with bay windows that were framed with pilasters, or columns, that protruded slightly from the wall, which then were aligned with beams in the ceiling. But most of the painting was of a spectacular staircase, which seemed to flow from a door near the ceiling to the floor.

"Is that a real place?" Sandra caught herself. "I mean, was that a real place?"

"Yes," said Van Lank. "When I was filling the shelves with my books it reminded me where my love of them started. And I mean real books, novels, paper and printed ink books, not digital ones."

"Anyway, I guess I never told you, but when I was younger a few of my college buddies and I went to Italy. In Florence we went into the San Lorenzo Church. Michelangelo designed it, and we heard it was an architectural masterpiece. Well, it is, I mean was, but I was really blown away by the vestibule to the Laurentian Library inside. The staircase design came to Michelangelo in a dream. It was this flowing design that seemed alive, that seemed to beckon me to climb it. And at the top is the reading room. Think of it, a room designed by one of the greatest Masters of all time, devoted entirely to books, to reading, one of the only things that man engages in that is both a method of learning and a relaxing pastime. From that minute on, I purchased all of my books in bound form and avoided the digital versions."

Sandra looked quickly around the room, her eyes settled on the media pad that was resting on a chest of drawers. "Are you going to tell me that if I look on your pad right now, I won't find any digital books?"

"Oh, I admit that if I can't find a bound copy of a book I want, I do purchase it through my e-reader app. But that's only as a last resort. Because real books have a heart, a soul."

Sandra scrunched her nose. "How do you mean?"

"Tell me," said Van Lank. "What are the titles of your favorite books on your pad?"

"Well, let me see," Sandra took a deep breath and sighed. "There's 'Quantitative Image Analysis', 'Directed Sequenching Strategy'..."

"Oh my God, stop, stop!" Van Lank was laughing. "Why don't you read something with maybe a bit of humanity in it? A novel perhaps."

"Be serious," said Sandra as she turned and made her way to the door. "I have a technically difficult job. How could a novel help me with that?"

Van Lank stepped towards her and rested his hands on her shoulders. He looked into her eyes. "Maybe by reawakening a part of you that I know still lives in your heart, before humans became just genomes to you and their thoughts and longings just chemical reactions."

"But that's what I do. I digitize people, reduce them to data."

Van Lank touched Sandra's nose lightly. "But we're more than that, aren't we?" He leaned in and placed a soft kiss on Sandra's lips.

"Maybe you were just born at the wrong time."

"I used to think that," reflected Van Lank. "But that was before I met you."

Van Link kissed Sandra more passionately. He then wrapped his arms around her and pulled her closer to him. Sandra squirmed a bit, looked over her shoulder out the door, and gently pulled herself away.

"How can you even think of that? The world's gone forever."

"A city," quoted Van Lank. "Becomes the world when you love one of its inhabitants. The same could be said of this ship."

Sandra contemplated the quote for a moment and smiled.

"It's from the 'Alexandria Quartet', a series of novels," explained Van Lank.

Sandra leaned forward and gave him a quick kiss on his lips. She started out the door and said, "Hey, Ryan. Keep reading."

And that was just five minutes ago and now here she was with her stomach in knots. She heard the door open behind her and the sound of Bennish's quick steps across the tiles. She was hidden from Bennish's view by her chair's high back and wraparound design, and for a few more seconds she could feel safe, like a moth caterpillar in a silk cocoon. But, unlike those clueless caterpillars, she knew that silk was cultivated by heating the cocoons and killing the moth, and already she could feel the heat from Bennish's grilling. She winced at the prospect.

Bennish spun her chair around. His jaw was set and his face boiled with anger. He had seen the red photos on the monitor and knew something was wrong. Something was wrong with 'his' mission. The one he was responsible for. He stared hard at Sandra, and a worm of distrust began to stir.

"What's going on here?"

"There's some corruption in the strands, sir. I'm running diagnostics now."

Bennish looked at Sandra, eyes glowering. Then the flames went out, the set jaw retracted, and the nostrils lost their flare. When Bennish spoke it was with distraction, as if he were late for an appointment…or had something better to do.

Sandra didn't know what caused the transformation, but she was thankful for it.

"Since it's only three strands I don't see it as a system wide emergency," Bennish said hurriedly. "Probably a problem with your bio-informatics. You should've stranded those three more carefully. Do what you have to do and report back to me in the morning. I'll be in my quarters if you need me, but I want everyone to turn in soon. Busy day tomorrow."

"Yes, sir."

That could be it, thought Sandra. Maybe I rushed through the stranding process, maybe my aim was off. There was a lot going on at the time with the emergency liftoff and everything. She was glad that Bennish now seemed unconcerned. Maybe she was making too big a deal of it.

Bennish turned and walked out of the room. Without looking back he said, "I thought you knew what you were doing."

9.
BENNISH

"Where the hell am I?"

Bennish was trying to focus his eyes on the sprinkler head directly above his bed. It would be crystal clear one second than fuzzy the next, as if someone was smearing Vaseline in his eyes after every blink. He closed them tightly and took inventory of the rest of his body.

He was suffering from the usual after affects. His sinus membranes had swelled, causing rhinitis, but that would be alleviated by his steroidal nose spray. The pharyngitis would be treated with Vicodin, as would the discomfort he was now experiencing in his hard palate.

As for the paregoric taste in his mouth, well, that was something that he had learned to live with. As a matter of fact, he liked it; it reminded him of childhood, when that toothless hick would rub it on his gums to soothe his teething pains. Such a shame that paregoric became regulated in the '70's; generations of kids had missed out on it!

Bennish opened his eyes again. The sprinkler's deflector plate and water nozzle came clearly into view. There, thought Bennish. Only took a few seconds.

Bennish rubbed his forehead. He cursed the previous day's early liftoff, it threw off his daily routine, his rituals, and that is not good for a user, an abuser. Missing his morning 'fix' caused him to feel irritable and angry the rest of the day. But looking back, Bennish thought he did okay. Sure he had some harsh words for Mac and Rott, but they had deserved it. And then right when he was heading to his room last night to finally nourish his need, Hapgood had called him to the data room. Why hadn't she gone to bed? God damn her!

But then Bennish remembered the corrupted strands and, like a warden enjoying the doomed prisoner's expression when told the Governor hadn't stayed the execution, took joy in Hapgood's predicament.

And it felt good, thought Bennish, seeing the prima donna swallow her pride, seeing her choke on it!

Bennish remembered leaving Hapgood and finally making it to his quarters and slamming the door shut behind him. Man, he had had enough for the day dealing with those whiney, weak kneed, know-it-all bastards. Thank God, he wouldn't have to face them again until morning.

Too bad they were nothing like the soldiers he had spent the best years of his life with. Those were good times. Driving his men mercilessly during the day, then drinking and whoring it up at night. The next morning he'd kick the strange bitches out of his bed.

Strange bitches. Bennish thought of Minami and Hapgood. Like one of Pavlov's dogs, he licked his lips at the prospects.

And Van Lank, that granola-crunching faggot, was getting a piece of Hapgood's tight little ass. Probably needs a pill to get it up. Oh well, maybe I'll nail that Minami chick. She'd probably fight back a little, but that would make it all the more gratifying. Man, the things I'd make her do, she'd be like a dog on a leash, obeying my every command or getting a swift slap across that cute little face of hers.

Bennish chuckled to himself.

Hell, she's so afraid of me she's probably thinking of coming over here right now and offering herself on a platter, hoping I'll then go easy on her. Yeah, I'll go easy on her, till I bang the shit out of her! No sir, never go easy on anyone, as my old man used to say.

My old man. Boy, now there was a tough son-of-a-bitch.

Bennish became melancholy. He rubbed the back of his head as he relived his memories.

Man, those beatings my old man would give me when he drank, or worse, when he drank and lost money playing hold'em with the guys. But the beatings gave me backbone. He respected me for being able to pull myself off the floor. Then he'd get me a wet rag to put on my bloodied lips and tell me I was a good kid, and that he had no idea how a kid as good as me came out of my no-good mother's -----.

But the time I hit him back, now that was something. Sixteen years old and I stood up to him, I did. Punched him right in the gut. Talk about fists of fury! He came at me with everything he had. We trashed that frigging living room, and if he hadn't caught me in the back of the head with that brass lamp, I know I would've kicked his ass.

Knocked me out cold. Then the old lady grabbed his arm as he was cocking it for the next blow and she lost a tooth for her troubles. Pop said she flew back about ten feet when he walloped her! Taught her to interfere in our business. And pop calling her a toothless hick after that. I loved that shit. The day she went from being 'my old lady' to the 'toothless hick'.

But Pop was right about her, I don't know how he knew, but he had pegged her as gutless. And time proved him right, by God. Anyone that takes a bottle of pills instead of putting a gun in their mouth is truly gutless.

But those formative years proved advantageous for Bennish once he was accepted at the Academy. He was tough and also a quick learner. He saw how some of the officers above him were able to move up the ladder while others languished. He studied their every move to see how much was due to merit, palm greasing, or the good ol' art of manipulation. Bennish was then able to combine all three into a formidable stick that he carried by his side throughout his career. Sometimes it was the stick he swung and other times it was the velvet-gloved hand he offered. Bennish had known whose ass to kiss and whose ass to kick. Military officer, politician, waitress, garbage-man, it didn't matter who Bennish had dealings with, he would manipulate, coerce or strong-arm that person in order to reach a personal goal. He once resorted to murder.

About two years ago, Bennish was scheduled for a bi-annual psyche evaluation. Bennish was so cunning, so good at manipulating people, that he had always passed the exam with flying colors. But this time, the examining physician was Dr. Earl Weintraub, and he literally wrote the book on Antisocial Personality Disorder, which is defined as the selfish, callous and remorseless use of others.

People with APD have a grandiose sense of self-worth, yet have no sense of empathy or feelings towards their fellow man. They fail to accept responsibility for their own actions and will stop at nothing to fulfill their own needs. And since most of the population can't spot these devils-in-human-clothing, a person afflicted with APD can prey on them easily. That was how, on Earth, handsome, seemingly socially fit serial killers were able to lure their unsuspecting victims like a child to candy.

Bennish wasn't stupid. He had seen other officers dismissed after their psyche exam and utilized all of his available resources to find out why. Not because he knew he suffered from APD, but because the predator in him did not want to be banned from the hunting ground. And if some of his prey had the ability to do that, it was a matter of self-preservation to discover how to neutralize the threat by eliminating the prey.

And it was with great sadness, that a week before Bennish's psyche exam was scheduled to take place, the Base Commander emailed a statement to all officers that the throttle in Dr. Weintraub's luxury sedan had malfunctioned, and he was killed in a crash that had shut down the interstate for hours. Bennish immediately replied with his own email, offering to coordinate a collection for a floral arrangement. And the elaborate white tulip and peach rose basket that Bennish chose was loved by the good doctor's family. Of course, Bennish had overcharged each contributor, and ended up making a few bucks on the deal.

And soon Bennish received the phone call stating that his psyche exam was going to be delayed a week. And when he finally met with Dr. Weintraub's replacement; a fresh-faced, inexperienced physician, he passed the exam with flying colors. So the sly fox, Bennish, was still free to play in the henhouse, which allowed him to pursue his next goal, the captain's chair of *Prometheus*.

Kalin Bennish was not going to be turned to ash by some bomb set off by a faceless enemy 3,000 miles away. No sir. If someone wanted to challenge him to a knife fight, or some other person-to-person combat, he'd have a chance of going out in a blaze of glory. So he'd accept the offer to fight to the death. Of course, he would make sure he'd stack the odds in his favor to ensure he won. Just like he made sure he was picked to lead *Prometheus*. Captain Segal was supposed to get the job. A good man, but a good man has one flaw. He doesn't see the world through the eyes of a social predator, so therefore can't see when he's being set up for failure.

Bennish had met General Avery Howard Bitner's wife, Hilary, at a social about two years ago. He immediately identified her as a woman craving attention, and Bennish knew he had an easy mark. Bennish had shown her kindness and wooed her with compliments. Within a month, he was bedding her and prodding her for information; innocent pillow talk which provided him with a wealth of knowledge. And one thing he found out, which he put in his vault until it could be put to use, was that General Bitner, the overweight, balding sixty year old man, was jealous of the suave, debonair Captain Segal. When Bennish heard this, a light went on in his head, but he doused it and promised himself it would shine brightly again one day if he ever needed Segal out of his way.

So, when Captain Segal was designated as leader of *Project Prometheus*, Bennish flipped the switch. He approached General Bitner in the canteen one day, knowing he'd be invited to sit and join him for lunch. Bennish made sure he steered the conversation toward Captain Segal's appointment and, just like he knew would happen, General Bitner asked Bennish's opinion.

"Captain Segal is a fine man, a fine man," Bennish plastered his face with a serious look. "And God knows it's going to be a tough job and men like Segal, and myself for that matter, like challenges, and he's fully up to the task." Bennish looked towards the ceiling for a second. He moved his head side to side as if he was having a silent argument with himself, and then whispered something as if he was convincing himself of the outcome. "Minami and Hapgood will be okay."

General Bitner was concerned. "What did you say, Captain?"

"Oh, I'm sorry, sir. Guess I was thinking out loud." Bennish looked down as if in remorse. "I know this mission is the most important one ever assembled, and its under your umbrella, sir, which means you're ultimately responsible, and you want everything to be perfect, but…"

"Spit it out man!" Bitner was getting anxious.

"Well, sir, it's like this. I don't know how to say it any other way. You see, Minami and Hapgood, well, sir, they are very intelligent, hard-working women. And I know how stress can affect women, sir. I told you my poor old mum committed suicide…" Bennish wiped an imaginary tear from his eye, "...because she couldn't take the pressure of life, even though my father and I did everything we could to help her." Bennish paused as if all the talk was out of him.

"Go on!"

"Well, General, sir, Captain Segal..." Bennish leaned in closer over the table. "Please don't tell him I said anything, sir, but Captain Segal has, how do I put this, an eye for the ladies..."

"Only natural for him. Good-looking bastard and he knows it. I'm sure he has them falling at his feet," said Bitner gruffly.

"The thing is, sir, is that I'm afraid he might make Commander Minami and Chief Scientific Officer Hapgood uncomfortable. Could affect their work. See, Segal told me he wanted to 'nail every good lookin' bitch' he saw. He said he didn't care if she was an officer, NCO, janitor, officer's wife..."

"Did he ever mention my Hilary?" asked Bitner, anger rising.

"Please, sir. I've said too much already..."

And the conversation followed the trail of deceit that Bennish had laid and by the time General Bitner had finished his plastic cup of chocolate pudding, Bennish was the leader of *Project Prometheus*.

And last night, as Bennish lay in his quarters, his mind started thinking. First of all, he was going to watch Rottweiler and MacNamara closely. They were too wise for their own good; he'd bring them down a few levels. He'd need to devise something cunning enough to really put the screws to them. And as for the corrupted strands, well, Hapgood better get that fixed. Every strand that was corrupted could mean one less human being re-instantiated when they landed, one less person in the new community. One less person he would rule over.

Bennish planned to see to it that he would be the leader of the New World. Yes, there were some people in stasis that would be formidable foes, and he'd have to deal with them. And yes, if some of their strands did become permanently corrupted, then they'd no longer be a threat. Hmmmmm. Wait a minute. The deletion of some strands could mean the deletion of some threats. So corruption of strand data was like a digital 'hit'!

Hit. Bennish shot up out of bed and slid his closet door aside so fast he almost tore it off its track. He reached up and behind some clothing on the top shelf and retrieved a small vile of brown liquid and a needle-less Transdermal Drug Delivery System (T.D.D.S.). About the size of a small caliber handgun, a T.D.D.S. delivers drugs by dispersing it through the skin by a strong burst of air.

Once the vile was inserted into the T.D.D.S., he carefully, ritualistically, withdrew a small amount of liquid into the glass chamber. Bennish then placed it down on his bed then picked up his wireless headphones. He placed them on his head and selected a song with a wild techno beat. He picked up the T.D.D.S. and started moving to the music, strutting around the room. When he'd see himself in the mirror, he'd hold the T.D.D.S. up in a two handed grip and aim at the reflection.

"Halt! You son-of-a-bitch!

As the music reached its crescendo, Bennish sat down on the foot of his bed. He looked over both shoulders, to center himself, and opened his mouth wide. He placed the muzzle of the T.D.D.S. against the roof of his mouth and engaged it. Almost simultaneously, the brown liquid disappeared and the T.D.D.S. hit the floor.

Bennish gasped once and trembled slightly as his eyes rolled back in his head. Then, as sadistic fantasies formed in a brain doused with enough hallucinogens to kill a horse, Bennish fell back on the bed.

And now, ten hours later, it was time to get up and face another day in this tin can.

Bennish got off his bed, took a second to steady himself, then searched the floor for the T.D.D.S. He placed it back on the shelf in plain view; he wanted to keep it handy, for he intended to use it much more frequently beginning today.

10.
ONE SMALL STEP

"It's got erectile dysfunction," exclaimed MacNamara as he studied a computer generated image (CGI) of the damaged thruster.

Bennish, Mac and Mineko were sitting in the cockpit, crowded around a monitor that displayed a CGI thruster emitting hot plasma gas. They had been observing it for about five minutes and comparing this graphical simulation with the data stream of text that was scrolling across the screen of another monitor.

"In English, please, MacNamara," grumbled Bennish.

"The thruster thinks its providing thrust when it isn't," translated Mineko. "It's generating two data streams. The graphical simulation looks fine, yet the text status screen is telling us it's not firing at all." Mineko took a deep breath and sighed. "Last night, they were both displaying intermittent function."

MacNamara had woken up early, grabbed two Thermos mugs of coffee, and headed up to the cockpit, where Mineko was already at her station. She accepted the mug gratefully. They both knew Bennish would be expecting a report first thing and they had scheduled this early morning rendez-vous the previous evening.

"Look at the CGI graphic compared to the text status screen," said Mineko as she pointed to a couple of monitors.

Mac leaned in to look at the CGI. The bill of his Red Sox cap struck the monitor so he spun the bill towards the back of his head.

"Do you ever not wear that cap?" asked Mineko.

"I raised Bassett Hounds," said Mac, seemingly avoiding the question. "The most slothful creatures on the planet. They even tried to outdo each other in laziness. One of them stopped eating. He preferred starving to chewing."

"Okay," said Mineko smiling. "And this relates to your cap how?"

"My father raised hounds too, and my grandfather before him. I spent my summers with my grandpa, he took me camping skiing, swimming, you name it. He taught me to love adventure, to embrace challenges."

"Sounds like a fine man."

"He was," said Mac, his usual jovial face now darkened with sadness. "Anyway, when his beloved Red Sox were in the World Series in 2004, it looked like they really had a chance to win it, which they hadn't done since 1918, and my grandpa had spent his whole life hoping to see it happen. The Sox were up three games to none and all they had to do was win one more game to clinch the series. Well, my grandpa had a heart attack the afternoon before the final game."

"Oh no. What a shame. And after all those-"

"Oh, the heart attack wasn't fatal, but grandpa had to stay in the hospital overnight. He had failing eyesight and my dad knew that he'd never be able to see the game on the thirteen inch TV's they had in hospital rooms back then, so my dad told grandpa we'd visit him that night and we left." Mac sat down in the co-pilot seat and leaned forward, excited to be able to relate this personal story to Mineko.

"We drove to an electronics store, where we bought a big screen TV. We then headed to Fenway Park, where we bought caps, hotdogs and bottles of Coke from sidewalk vendors. We went back to the hospital and set everything up in grandpa's room while he napped." Mac let out big guffaw as he relived the moment. "Man, you should've seen his face when he woke up. We sat there together and watched the Red Sox win the Worlds Series, one of the happiest days of my life. I was happy for my grandpa mostly."

The smile on Mac's face slowly turned downward, as if someone were turning a knob on the back of his head. "Grandpa died a week later. My dad buried him with the cap I wore that night and he gave me this one, the one my grandpa was wearing." Mac took a deep breath. His eyes lit back up and smiled broadly. "Does that answer your question?"

"Yes," said Mineko. "And thank you for sharing your story."

"Thank you for listening."

And now Mac and Mineko were looking at Bennish expectantly, awaiting his orders regarding the erroneous thruster readings.

Bennish rubbed his face with both hands. "Okay. No more wasting time. Mac, you're going for a post-apocalyptic walk outside. We need visual confirmation. I'll have Hapgood help you suit up." Bennish waved his hand at the monitor displaying the CGI animation. "We're not going to put our faith in a damn cartoon."

"Right, Captain."

Mac left the flight deck, turned towards the elevator doors, and pressed the call button. Once inside, he engaged a button for a floor only two stories down; not the eighty stories that would place him in the airlock closest to the thrusters. The only reason he didn't bypass the elevator completely was because Bennish would've tore into him if he were caught taking the slow way down. Mac was proud of his athleticism; he had been a star football player at Purdue, and exercised his body whenever he could.

Mac stepped off the elevators and made for the stairwell. He figured it would take him about eleven minutes to traverse the seventy-eight flights of stairs to the thruster air lock. This would be his second good workout in the last twenty-four hours.

The previous night, in his quarters, he had engaged in strenuous exercise thanks to his Virtual Reality Generator. By projecting three-dimensional holographic images, the shoebox sized V.R. Generator could replicate sights, sounds and sensations such as wind, heat and cold. And last night, MacNamara had utilized it for all its worth. Well, almost all its worth; he had kept the volume to a minimum.

The V.R. Generator was one of the 'banned' items that the crew was supposed to have stored in one of the ship's warehouses along with photographs and digital media players/recorders. The psychiatrists believed that it would be best if the crew concentrated solely on their chores. They postulated that perusing photos or home movies would be counter-productive, resulting in an air of melancholy permeating the ship. As a matter of fact, there was even some debate regarding music, as certain songs can trigger intense memories and emotions.

But cooler heads prevailed and at least the crew had been allowed to keep music and reading materials on their pads. And Sandra Hapgood, since she would be the last person to enter stasis, was entrusted with the Human History Computer so that she could continually add entries to the device, right up until she had to strand herself. Mac still found it amazing that the entire history of humankind, along with digital files of blueprints, books, manuals, etc. required the same sized digital storage space, about twenty zetabytes, as just one human being's strand.

Mac chuckled at the thought of it. You could hold all of human history in the palms of your hands, yet the strand data of five thousand odd subjects' required the processing and storage power of five thousand, full sized, networked computers and servers. Of course, once the ship landed and the subjects were re-instantiated, the computers would be released from their duty and would be available for the subject's own use. And since they were available in all shapes and sizes, from desktops to pads, subjects could pick the one best suited to their educational or professional needs. The history computer would then be joined to the network, and its data made available to all.

And once the crewmembers were able to claim their computers, Mac would fess up to having the V.R. Generator hidden away in his room. For now, he'd use it only when Bennish ordered lights out. Then, like last night, he'd place the unit in the corner of his quarters and punch in the environment he wanted to replicate.

Parachuting in the Himalayan mountains, that's what Mac had 'experienced' the previous evening. The V.R. Generator projected a virtual world all around him, sky, mountains, even the Fishtail Air AS 350 B3 helicopter that dropped him from the world's highest drop zone, Gorak Shep, Kala Patthar Plateau. The V.R. Generator tracked Mac's movements in its holographic world, so that it could orient him correctly in its virtual space, and project his parachute and gear on to his body. The illusion was so precise and real that Mac could even grab for a virtual emergency rip-cord on his virtual vest if he had programmed the V.R. Generator for a failed chute scenario.

But last night, Mac had 'landed' on Everest, then, magically, skis had appeared on his feet and he had slalomed his way right to the mountain's base. It felt so real that Mac wanted to head to a ski lodge and have a hot cup of cocoa when he reached the base of the mountain!

Mac thought about the first, crude video game system that could read a person's movements and translate them into a virtual setting. He had been seventeen years old and had purchased a new attachment for his existing game system. It had an integrated camera and sensors, and though it didn't always work, and even when it did, it couldn't read all of his movements correctly, he enjoyed it immensely. That is, of course, until the unit was pulled from the market about a year later. Apparently, hackers figured out a way to tap into the manufacturer's servers and 'peek' into the living rooms and homes of the consumers.

A series of class action lawsuits kept the manufacturer tied up in court battles for years. And once it was discovered that the manufacturer itself was spying on consumers in order to assist its Marketing Department, the gavel came down hard. The manufacturer was fined heavily and lost the business, and more importantly, the faith of consumers that believed in their right to privacy.

Mac had to laugh. The famous philanthropist that Rott had riled against in their meeting earlier had been the head of that company. He had lost a small fortune. Oh well, guess his philanthropic contributions were just a way to obtain a big write-off, thought Mac as he stepped out of the stairwell, refreshed from the exertion of his descent.

"How nice of you to finally show up." Sandra was leaning against the hull directly opposite the stairwell door. She smiled and put a hand up to her mouth, as if suppressing a yawn.

Mac mocked a bow and tipped his ever-present cap. "Sorry to keep m'lady waiting," Mac winked. "But I wanted to let you enjoy the anticipation of seeing me in skivvies as long as possible."

"Isn't there an old saying that sometimes the anticipation is better than the actual event?" Sandra volleyed back.

"Hey, you sound like my ex-girlfriends!"

They both laughed as they entered the anteroom to the airlock. Twelve spacesuits and their associated helmets lined one wall. The opposite wall was lined with shelves stacked with equipment. The far wall had one large door, surrounded by an inflated black rubber ring. This was the entrance to the airlock. Sandra grabbed a spacesuit that was marked '*MacNamara*' in embroidered script and proceeded to loosen its fasteners as Mac stripped down to his underwear. He then zipped on a one-piece, elastic body suit that resembled footed pajamas.

"Where's my nightcap?" joked Mac.

"You'll have to settle for a ten pound fishbowl," Sandra replied as she pointed to the row of helmets.

"I guess that will have to do," replied Mac as he stepped into the spacesuit one leg, then one arm, at a time.

Sandra zipped the suit up then flattened the Velcro flap against its opposite member, covering the zipper with this secondary fastener. "What do you think you'll find out there?"

"I'm not sure what to think," said Mac reflectively as he proceeded to put on his boots and gloves. "It's generating conflicting feedback so the thruster itself could be fine and we may just be dealing with damaged sensors." Mac paused as he stood up and stomped his feet and tugged on each glove. "That's what I'm hoping for anyway. We're not really equipped to make major repairs; that's why this ship has four thrusters. It can fly with only one. Not efficiently, mind you, but we could do it."

Mac stooped down and turned his cap's visor around so that Sandra could place the helmet over his head. Once the helmet clicked into position, she slid the retainer latch to lock it in place. "Okay, let's light up this Christmas tree." Mac flicked a switch on the suit's control panel, which was on his left forearm, and a series of status lights and control buttons glowed lime green.

"Well that's a good sign," said Mac as he grabbed a Portable Oxygen and Transportation Unit (P.O.T.U.) off the opposite wall.

The P.O.T.U. was, literally, the size of a breadbox and was covered with little nozzles; all pointing in various directions. With small bursts of propellant from these nozzles, an astronaut would be able to maneuver himself in space. It also contained the astronaut's air supply. Mac checked the propellant and oxygen gauges and, satisfied that both were full, slid the unit on his back like a knapsack. After securing the oxygen feeder hose to the suit's port near his shoulder, he grabbed a securing strap in each hand and mated the thick, plastic clasps together at his sternum.

Sandra tugged on the P.O.T.U. to ensure it was secure. "That's not going anywhere." She then pressed the large red button on the wall. The thick rubber ring around the inner airlock door deflated and the door slid open. "But you are!"

* * *

"What a rush!" thought Mac as he floated over the hull of the ship.

Once Sandra had shut the inner airlock door behind him, Mac turned to the outer door, the three inches of ceramisteel and Lexan that separated him from space. He started to mildly hyperventilate. Not because of nervousness or fear but because he was so excited. In Mac's mind, spacewalking, even at its slow, plodding pace, was more exciting than parasailing, skiing, or skydiving. Perhaps it was because his V.R. Generator couldn't duplicate the experience correctly. And how could it? Half the excitement of space walking was the danger, though miniscule, of becoming permanently separated from the ship.

In the early days of space travel, astronauts tethered themselves with umbilical and safety cords, but with the advent of the P.O.T.U, those lifelines became unnecessary. In addition, those lifelines had their own drawbacks: their finite length and permanent tethering of the suit to the ship limited maneuverability. Mac was glad to be free of those restrictions. He chomped at the bit to exit the ship and experience that wonderfully liberating feeling of flying, something that most humans had only experienced in their dreams.

Mac's gloved hand depressed the large button and the outer airlock door opened silently. Due to the absence of all background noise in the vacuum of space, the sound of his breathing became clearly evident. "Mac to control. I'm stepping out." Bennish's voice came back clearly through the helmet's speakers. "Roger that, Mac."

The first step out of the ship was always the best. Mac was always reminded of an old Indiana Jones movie, where Harrison Ford had to step off a cliff into what looked like thin air. But it was a 'step of faith' he was to take, and when the Indiana character took the step, he was shocked to find that he landed on a stone walkway that had been hidden from view due to an optical illusion. Well, when Mac stepped out of the ship, his feet didn't hit anything solid, and neither did the rest of his body. He had pushed off a bit with the toes of his boots and this small motion was enough to separate him from the safety of the ship and propel him into space. He was a baby leaving the womb. And now he was floating away from the steel womb, toward its aft, or tail end, in the direction of the impaired thruster.

Mac had judged the push off from the airlock perfectly. He was travelling about two feet per second and his momentum would peter out in about thirty more. His speed and trajectory would ultimately place him about forty feet above the troubled thruster. This would be the perfect vantage point, as he'd be able to see the extent of damage the thruster suffered when the shrapnel hit it on liftoff.

Mac extended his arms straight out and 'flew' the last few yards like a superhero out to save a damsel in distress. And once he slowed to a halt, he pulled his arms back to a neutral position, assumed an almost seated pose, and then became the consummate professional as he stared intently at the thruster. For a few seconds he was as still as a statue, The Thinker without the stone seat. But those few seconds, in conjunction with Mac's eye for detail, provided a wealth of information.

"Mac to *Prometheus*. Clear view of thruster and surrounding area. Something sliced through the housing, left a clean hole about two meters square. All plasma conduits and exchangers are A-OK. A couple of power line feeds have been torn, and the power management feedback terminal is literally sliced in half."

"Are you sure you don't see anything else?" queried Bennish.

"Positive. And this confirms what we've seen on the ship. The thruster is firing, but the CGI animation isn't getting proper feedback. And with a few power lines out of commission, that explains our power stores being down a bit."

"Okay, Mac. If you're sure you don't need to examine anything else, bring it in."

Mac twisted his body so that he faced the open, outer airlock door, about forty feet away. He engaged one of the glowing thruster controls on his left forearm. Immediately, a plastic ring around the cuff of his left glove glowed with a series of green lights. His gloved hand became the P.O.T.U. controller and by squeezing his hand into a fist and twisting it to and fro, he would cause propellant to flow in small bursts from the various nozzles, propelling him in any direction necessary.

The job is over, thought Mac. No one can see me, why not have some fun? Mac decided against heading directly for the airlock door. He had a better idea.

Mac placed his body parallel to the ship's hull, which was about thirty feet away. He looked towards the open airlock door, then at a spot thirty feet above it. That would be his target. Mac planned to engage the thrusters on his P.O.T.U. so that he'd fly forward approximately forty feet. Then right as he hit the target, a position thirty feet above the open airlock door, he would engage all of the P.O.T.U.'s rear facing nozzles simultaneously. This 'kick in the back' would abruptly change his direction, breaking his forward momentum and flinging him towards the airlock entrance. Right as he entered the ship, he'd spin around and let off one more P.O.T.U. burst. If all went well, he'd stop right at the inner airlock door. At best, he'd bump it gently. At worst he'd bend a few of the rear nozzles. So what? There were eleven more P.O.T.U.s on board.

Mac looked at his target spot and he flexed his left hand to get it ready for the maneuvers he would soon have to make in quick fashion. He allowed his eyes to look past the target and follow the hull of the ship all the way up to the cockpit some hundred stories away. My God, the length of the ship seemed endless. It made him feel small, miniscule. For a second he lost his nerve. What if the P.O.T.U. fails? What if I can't make the turn? What if I keep going straight, watching the letters of *Prometheus* flash by in reverse order until I pass the windows of the cockpit and see Bennish and Mineko staring at me, mouths open, knowing I'm going to be lost in space forever?

They'd be no hope of retrieval, thought Mac. The ship wasn't designed for tight maneuvers. Once the engines lit up, it'd have to travel about five hundred miles before it could stop. And its turning radius was fifty miles. No matter how many times they'd try to loop by and get me it would be futile; like trying to catch a fly with chopsticks while speeding by on a motorcycle. My oxygen would soon run out and I'd die a horrible death, only to become a satellite, a dead moon to one of these sterile, lifeless planets, sealed in my 'Made in USA' polyester/cotton/copper weaved coffin. For the love of God, what have I done, what am I doing out here?

Mac mentally slapped himself. Get a hold of yourself! You're not a schoolboy on some carnival ride crying for your mommy to pull you off. You do this all the time. You thrive and live for being on the edge. Now focus on the target and engage the nozzles! Let's bring this baby home.

Mac concentrated on the target, clenched his fist, and twisted his hand. The nozzles in the bottom of the P.O.T.U, the ones that faced his feet and the rear of the ship, released a burst of propellant that sent him forwards. The gaping black hole of the entrance was coming up quickly beneath him. Steady now, don't engage the thruster yet. Hold it. Hold it. Now!

Mac twisted his hand to engage the rear nozzles. Nothing happened! Mac overshot the target spot. The air-lock opening flashed by below him. Mac furiously clenched and twisted his fist. The P.O.T.U. didn't respond. Mac had a $200,000 useless brick on his back. And as the black, twenty-foot tall letter 'S' entered his field of view, Mac swallowed hard, trying to loosen the grip of fear that had taken hold of his vocal cords. The quivering in his voice betrayed the forced humor in the tough, devil-may-care, throwaway line that Mac thought would be expected of him.

"Houston, we have a problem."

11.
HELPING HAND

Phfffffffttttt...

Sandra let go of the P.O.T.U.'s manual burst control switch. Empty!

When Sandra heard Mac's transmission, she immediately tore at one of the hanging spacesuits and proceeded to suit up as she listened to the panicked conversation between Bennish and Mac.

"What kind of problem?"

"My P.O.T.U's shit the bed. I'm flying over the ship, aft to forward, about two feet per second."

"Can you get your feet near the hull?"

Sandra had put on her helmet, not an easy feat to perform solo, and was now reaching for a P.O.T.U. Bennish was trying to be helpful; suggesting Mac's magnetized boot soles might be able to slow him down, but she knew that would have been the first thing Mac would try if he was close enough to the hull.

"Negative. I'm a good thirty feet above it."

"Can you pull off your air hose and use it for propulsion?"

"Negative. Once it's disconnected it shuts down."

"Hapgood. Suit up." Commanded Bennish.

"I am."

"How long before you can exit the ship and get a visual?"

Sandra grabbed a P.O.T.U. The fuel level read 'full'. Sandra began to sling it on but thought better of it and engaged the control switch. A short burst of propellant escaped then puttered out. Sandra flung the unit to the floor and snatched at the next one.

"Hapgood?'

Sandra tested the second P.O.T.U. It failed also.

"Hapgood, goddammit, how long before you get out there? We haven't got all goddamn day!"

"Shit! None of the P.O.T.U.s work!"

Both Mac and Bennish replied simultaneously. "What do you mean?"

"What I said. The P.O.T.U.s are empty; no propellant."

"How the fuck?" screamed Bennish. "Rottweiler said all internals were working. That son-of-a-bitch."

But Sandra didn't hear Bennish's rant. She was staring at the floor; doing the math, weighing the odds. She said in a calm voice, "I'm going to get Mac."

"You stay the fuck where you are!" demanded Bennish.

"We're losing him," said Sandra. "And I can't talk right now." It was time to put her plan into action. She got down on one knee, like a gambler about to roll the dice in a sidewalk game of 'Craps', and reached for the nearest P.O.T.U. It was a desperate plan, the odds were long but the payoff was worth it. She grabbed another P.O.T.U.

"Stay on this ship, Hapgood, and that's an order. We can't lose you too."

Mac interjected. "Sandra don't, it's not worth it. I appreciate the thought."

But Sandra was already back on her feet and heading into the airlock.

* * *

"Mac. Turn around and face me"

Mac was now about two thirds of the way towards the ship's nosecone. The letter 'M' loomed beneath him. He had abandoned the flying position and now stood perpendicular to the ship, his arms and legs spread out, like Da Vinci's Vitruvian Man, in a desperate attempt to optimize resistance and slow his progress.

"Where are you?"

"Just turn around."

Cautiously, deliberately, Mac twisted his body in a slow-motion pirouette. He was now facing the rear of the ship while moving towards the nosecone at a rate of one foot per second. About fifty yards away, Mac could see the partial outline of a spacesuit against the backdrop of the ship's smooth, pearl-like skin. Like a scarecrow in a field of corn, only the torso, head and arms broke the surface. It was Sandra, the upper half of her body jutted out from the airlock entrance and she was waving.

"Mac. Listen carefully. I want you to unhook the airhose, undo the clasp, and take the P.O.T.U off."

"What? I won't be able to breathe."

"It's the only thing heavy enough to use as a counter-weight. You know that."

"But I won't be able to breathe!"

Bennish voice cut in sharply. "Hapgood, what the fuck are you trying to do out there?"

"It's the only way," said Sandra firmly. "If he takes the P.O.T.U off, faces the nose of the ship and pushes it away from himself with enough force, he'll be pushed back towards me." Sandra's voice softened. "Mac, please, it'll only take a minute. You can hold your breath longer than that. Every second we waste means you'll have to hold your breath longer. C'mon Mac. One small breath for man…one giant push for MacNamara!"

As if a switch had been flipped, Mac flew into action. He unclasped the securing straps, pulled the P.O.T.U gingerly off his back, so as not to kink the air hose, and held it in front of him. Then he pirouetted once more so that he now faced the nose of the ship, his direction of travel.

"Now Mac," pleaded Sandra. "You'll have to pull the P.O.T.U. as close to you as possible then push it away with all your might. So once you detach your air hose push the P.O.T.U. off at a five-degree angle. If you come in too steep, you'll hit the hull and bounce off before your boots can get hold. If you come in too high or wide, you'll be worse off than you are now. Five degrees will do it. As long as you come close to me, I'll catch you."

Mac took a series of deep breaths then held the last one. He quickly detached the air hose then, with one giant heave, pushed the P.O.T.U. away from himself. But one of the large plastic clasps caught on his hand for a second and the angle of the push off was compromised. The P.O.T.U flew upwards, away from the ship instead of almost parallel to it, tumbling and turning over itself into the blackness of space. Mac was flung backwards towards the hull. He looked down at the letters flying by beneath him.

-M-E-T-H-E-

It was all wrong. The letters were getting larger awfully quickly.

"Shit," said Sandra. "He's coming in too steep!"

Mac turned to face the rear of the ship, hoping his magnetized soles would grasp the hull but, to his horror, the ship was now only a few inches away. His knees struck the ceramisteel skin and he bounced off, rolling and somersaulting like a diver showboating off the high board. He was now heading away from the ship and would pass directly over Sandra, about thirty feet above her.

"Hapgood?" queried Bennish.

"Mac's heading away from the ship. I have to get him."

"Don't you dare! Let him go!"

Ship. Stars. Space. Sandra. Ship. Stars. Space. Sandra.

The kaleidoscope of images that were flashing by Mac as he twisted through space was disconcerting. There was no up, no down. Just the uncontrollable spin. His resourcefulness, his luck for getting himself out of jams that would paralyze normal men with sheer terror, was over.

Hadn't he once punched a shark in the nose at Glenelg Beach? Didn't he manually pull his reserve chute just a few thousand feet over Interlaken? And now he was a helpless rag doll, tumbling in the front load washer, looking out the circular glass door, the glass front of the helmet, at the repeating scene: Ship. Stars. Space. Sandra.

Wait a moment. Something in the scene had changed. Yes, that was it. Sandra was now coming out of the ship, heading towards him with arms outstretched. But the P.O.T.U.s! They didn't have propellant. She too would be lost in space forever. "Sandra, don't!" Mac wanted to scream. But the instinct to live, the subconscious part of the human mind that held out hope, wouldn't let him release the lungful of air.

Their two bodies met forcibly. The glass shield of Mac's helmet was whacked by Sandra's shield. Their heads snapped away from each other, like two billiard balls colliding on the green baize. But he was aware of Sandra's smiling face behind her shield and the sensation of her arms wrapping around him. Unfortunately, he was also aware that they were both still traveling away from the ship. They were going to die together. But why in God's name was Sandra smiling?

He knew half the answer when they suddenly jerked to a stop. He knew the other half when he looked down past Sandra towards the airlock entrance. For now he knew how Sandra had saved him. One of her P.O.T.U.'s straps was clasped to the strap of another P.O.T.U, which was then clasped to another P.O.T.U, all the way into the ship. As Mac studied this lifeline, this second chance at life, composed of multiple straps, Sandra looked at him, at the straps, and with a gleam in her eye said, "Strands."

12.
DIVIDED WE FALL

Van Lank, his body wound like a spring, sat stock still, head tilted to one side, like a dog anticipating the mailman. He had a lump in his throat caused by fear. Fear that Sandra was going to risk her own life to save MacNamara, as he, Van Lank, sat helplessly here in the Planet Assessment Room. He was following the unfolding drama over the intercom. The white grill of its flush mounted speaker, set high in the wall, was his focal point. If not for his synthetic fiber clothing and the banks of computers, monitors and electronic equipment that surrounded him, he could've easily been mistaken for an early 20th century homeowner, engrossed in the serials or newscasts emanating from an old time radio.

Once Sandra spoke those beautiful words, 'I've got Mac, I'm bringing him in', the coil in Van Lank began to unwind, the lump in the throat lessened. When he let out the pent up breath, it whistled threw his teeth. "Thank God!" he said aloud.

Mission Specialist Ryan Van Lank was once described by an ex-girlfriend, who dabbled in poetry, as 'a human vessel filled with a mixture of kindness, intelligence, and strong resolve. A wonderful elixir made even more palatable by a slight, muscular build, and handsome yet boyish face.' Everyone liked Van Lank. He was usually the calming influence of any group he joined, the oil that could still turbulent waters.

When the *Project Prometheus* team members were thrown together to conceive, design, and implement the most important mission ever attempted by humankind, the test of wills, the clashes of egos, and the stress filled atmosphere strained the fabric of cooperation. Van Lank patched the holes of mistrust and ironed out differences amongst the crew, all in hope of acting like the release valve of a pressure cooker. Yet Van Lank had one of the most stressful responsibilities of all. He would be the first human re-instantiated once a carbon-based, life-supporting planet was detected. It would be his judgment call, his decision, if the *Prometheus* should land or continue on its quest.

If the planet was not viable, Van Lank could end up sitting alone, the only human not in any form of statis (a second stranding could result in permanent amnesia), on a ship that could still have a four, five or six year voyage ahead of it. The experience would probably drive him mad and, if the proper answers weren't entered correctly into the weekly Mental Stability Test in the Behavioral Health Lab, the computer would immediately (and permanently) lock the doors, extract all oxygen from the room, and essentially murder Van Lank.

Van Lank reflected on the irony of it. If the computer 'neutralized' him due to his own poor programming, would that be murder or suicide?

Van Lank shrugged his shoulders. He liked the pressure. Since *Prometheus* would choose a planet based on the criteria he programmed into its scanners, the fear of it choosing a sub-par planet pushed him to an almost obsessive cycle of checking and rechecking his data. And that was what he had been doing, until Mac's plea for help broke his concentration like an alarm clock. And now the intercom came to life once more. It was Bennish's voice, and the undertone of menace could not be mistaken. "Everyone to the Ready Room. Now!"

* * *

"Someone bled the propellant from all of the P.O.T.U.s!"

MacNamara slammed a P.O.T.U. onto the table then stared into each of his seated crewmembers' eyes. He leaned forward and placed his palms on the table. He appeared ready to vault over it and tackle anyone that gave off even a hint of being guilty. "I ran an atmospheric in the air lock bay. Propellant everywhere. Someone bled it out of the P.O.T.U.s and reset the gauges to full."

Bennish turned to Rottweiler accusingly. The other crewmembers followed suit.

"What are you all looking at?" Rott looked right and left as he felt all eyes on him. It was disconcerting. The other crewmembers were looking at him like a jury in a courtroom, waiting for the defendant to explain himself.

But the distant look in Bennish's eye was different. It was the eye of the judge that had already convicted and sentenced the defendant, the executioner that was contemplating the rope, the chair or the injection.

"Weren't the P.O.T.U.s your responsibility?" queried Bennish.

"I checked the fuel and oxygen levels in all of them last night," said Rott defensively.

"You checked them manually?" asked Mac angrily.

"I trusted the gauges. That's what they're for!" explained Rott.

"Extinction is what we do. Isn't that what you said?" queried Mineko.

Before Rott could answer, Mac leaned across the table, grabbed him by his collar, and dragged him up and out of his seat. "You son-of-a-bitch!" Mac pulled his right hand back and balled it into a fist. Rott instinctively covered his face.

Instantly, everyone else was out of his and her seats, their hands grasping at the two men. They held Mac's fist back while loosening the grip of his other hand from Rott's collar.

"Hey now! Let's not jump to any conclusions." Van Lank had hopped over the table and was now squeezing himself between Mac and his intended punching bag.

"He tried to kill me!" stammered Mac.

"You don't know that," interjected Sandra.

"Well who else could've done it?" said Mac.

Van Lank held his hands up like a cop stopping traffic from two opposite directions. "Hold it. Everyone just hold it. Let's sit down and think this out logically."

A standoff as everyone just stood and stared at one another. Bennish, who had seemed to be enjoying the breakdown in camaraderie, finally spoke up. "Sit down everyone. Let's see if Rott can talk himself out of this one."

Rott straightened out his shirt and sat down, his face bright red with anger. "I don't have to talk myself out of anything."

"Listen," Van Lank said in a calm voice. "Rottweiler's not the only person that could've sabotaged the P.O.T.U.s. The ground crew had access to the ship for days before it was locked down."

"You think NASA was infiltrated?" asked Sandra.

"The Chrysander had people everywhere," said Mineko. "Devout followers, paid informants. He could talk some people into anything. He had that powerful personality."

Personality my ass, thought Sandra. About a year ago, when Sandra had first joined *Project Prometheus*, one of Sandra's best friends, Suzie Martel, had invited her out for the night. Suzie was an agent of Homeland Security and it was her job to keep tabs on The Chrysander. He was going to be speaking at the Ivan Legnad Senior Center in Rockledge, about fifteen miles from NASA. Suzie's intel predicted that in addition to about thirty senior citizens, there would be an additional forty to fifty young adults attending. Suzie knew that Sandra was curious how one man could enlist so many devout followers, so she offered Sandra the chance to see and hear the man in person.

Project Prometheus was in its infant stage and was still top secret, but that didn't stop Sandra from taking every precaution against recognition. She asked Suzie to disguise her, and her request rewarded her with a total makeover.

A blonde wig hid her black hair; blue contacts covered her brown eyes, and a padded 'weight adjustment suit' added what looked like forty pounds to her lithe frame. Even Sandra didn't recognize herself in the mirror.

Suzie picked up Sandra in her sleek, black convertible and they put on the air of a couple of carefree young women out on a Thursday night. They drove across the Bennett Causeway, laughing and joking, Sandra breathing in the cool night air deeply and enjoying every second of this, her first night away from the NASA compound.

Once in Rockledge, they had fajitas and one disciplined margarita each at the El Charro, then made their way to the Cozy Slumber Motel on Florida Avenue. "The senior center's parking lot will be packed," offered Suzie as she pointed at a low hung building behind a line of trees across the street.

"That's it there, entrance on the opposite side. A couple of other agents will park in this lot also. We don't think The Chrysander's people have made us or our vehicles, but it's better to play it safe and keep out of sight."

Sandra and Suzie exited the car, crossed the street, and made their way around to the entrance, where Suzie's words proved prescient; for there was a massive tie up in the lot as cars fought for non-existent spaces, and the lobby area was overflowing with people, most of them desperately trying to obtain a ticket. But the two young women had theirs and, once they accepted the brochures from the smiling young lady, they fought their way through the gauntlet of attendees and found their seats in the last row. The thick, stifling air was filled with palpable anticipation from the enthusiastic crowd.

"Man, it's hot in here," said Suzie.

"You think so?" said Sandra with mock sarcasm. "How do you think I feel? Sitting here under a hot wig and fat suit!"

Suzie laughed heartily. "Tell you what, I'll grab us a couple of drinks. What would you like?"

Sandra had caught a glimpse of the refreshment table on the way in. It groaned under the buckets of ice that held bottles and cans of water, soda, beer and energy drinks. Sandra was leaning towards an iced cold bottle of water. She said so.

"Oh, so I have to drink alone?" said Suzie merrily. "We never get a chance to see each other, and the firm doesn't mind if I drink a bit on duty 'cause they want us to act naturally, so how about having a beer with me?"

"All right," said Sandra. "You know what I like."

"That a girl." Suzie got up and made her way to the back of the room while Sandra examined her surroundings.

This must be the recreation room, thought Sandra, for the shelves on the wall were full of board games and the electronic whiteboard was still displaying the pros and cons of reverse mortgages; probably the musings of a financial advisor that had volunteered his time with the seniors that day.

The room had been filled with aluminum folding chairs, each one occupied, and there were still about twenty people at the refreshment table that would have to stand for the event. For a second, Sandra entertained the idea of calling the local fire department and reporting an occupancy code violation, which would certainly result in the cancellation of the night's proceedings. But this would be an act of folly

117

on Sandra's part, for she wanted to hear The Chrysander, wanted to see how he was able to sway people to his side, to his view, that humankind had ruined this planet and had no right to ruin another.

Her thoughts were interrupted as her heart skipped a beat, thanks to Suzie touching the back of her neck with an ice-cold beer bottle. Sandra turned around and grabbed it. Suzie held her bottle out. "To us and our first night out in months!" toasted Suzie. Sandra clicked her bottle against Suzie's. "To us!"

Both women took a long swig of the cold brew. As Suzie took her seat, the lights flashed and a hush blanketed the room. The Chrysander stepped on stage and there was polite applause. Good, thought Sandra, some people here haven't bought into his crap, they're probably here out of curiosity like I am.

"Ladies and gentlemen, thank you so much for coming out here tonight. I know some of you asked my sponsors why I didn't host this event at one of the larger auditoriums in the area or even the civic center, which would have allowed us to extend our invitation to many more of you, but I believe in intimacy. Something I can't obtain via my blogs or podcasts."

Sandra was bored already. She could not find anything attractive about this man, physically or mentally, that could explain his proven track record of recruiting members to his cause. She looked around the room. Some attendees were holding onto each of his words as a drowning man will grasp his lifesaver. Puh-lease, thought Sandra. Get a life. She took a long draught of her beer and looked at Suzie, who rolled her eyes but went back to listening. Hell, thought Sandra, it's Suzie's job, not mine. It's going to be a long night. She took another draught. Hey, you wanted to come, you wanted to hear the man. You're here now so listen to him.

Concentration proved difficult due to the heat of the wig and suit, the alcoholic drink, and the over taxed air conditioning system. Sandra took another long draught of the beer and drained the bottle. She listened again to The Chrysander's speech, but his monotone voice was the audible equivalent of paint drying. Within a minute, she was asleep.

Two hours later, Suzie shook Sandra's arm gently. She hoped to wake her without causing a scene. "Come on," whispered Suzie wearily. "It's over. You got to sleep through it. You lucky bastard! I was bored to tears!"

Sandra shook her head. Her mouth was dry, had she been snoring? "I'm sorry Suze, I couldn't take anymore. He's one of the most boring men I've ever seen in my life. Hopefully his star will fade and in a few months he'll be a footnote in history."

And now, twelve months later, Sandra's words had been proven wrong. The Chrysander became even more famous, more infamous. John Lennon had once made a remark, misconstrued by some, that The Beatles were more famous than Jesus. Well, the entire population of Earth had been aware of The Chrysander's 'teachings'. He ultimately became more famous than Jesus, Moses, Isaiah, Buddha, Confucius, Mohammed, and about ten other religious leaders, combined!

So Mineko was partly correct. The Chrysander had 'the power', but not because of his magnetic personality.

"You know," said Sandra as she addressed her fellow crewmembers, now in the present. "I had a friend in Homeland Security. She once told me that they suspected The Chrysander used drugs, brainwashing, behavorial modification, all that shit, to get people to do his bidding. They couldn't assassinate him, he would've become a martyr, and they couldn't subvert his followers, they were beyond loyal. She ended up quitting in disgust; his power over people was so strong. So yes, it's possible NASA was infiltrated."

"Well I'm not under anyone's influence except myself. And I did nothing wrong," said Rottweiler.

"The point is," said Sandra. "That you might not even know it if you were."

As those words hung in the air and the others digested them, all the lights in the room flashed off then on again.

"Are you kidding me?" snarled MacNamara.

"The power cut in and out," said Mineko.

"Rottweiler, check all power sources and see what the hell is going on," said Bennish. "I'll check in with you in thirty minutes. Hapgood, you better go check on the strands. Everyone else get back to your posts. I'll be damned if things start rolling downhill under my watch."

Everyone filed out of the room, each with their own private thoughts, fears, and suspicions swirling in their minds.

13.
A FOX IN THE HENHOUSE

"Now what the hell?"

Rott stood in the entrance of the Power Management Room, his jaw open. He did not expect to see what he was seeing: a thin film of iridescent fungus coating every square inch of equipment. The sixteen power storage cells, each the size of a tractor-trailer, glowed under the halogen lights like giant rectangular pearls. Their white ceramic skins shimmered with beautiful transparent ribbons of pink and turquoise. The black, rubber-coated interconnecting cables, thick as tree trunks, exhibited an oily sheen, as if dipped in liquid black gold. And the now moist, slippery, gray floor tiles mirrored everything in the room.

The eight-ounce spray bottle of Nutroxen, a disinfectant, and the sponge that he held in his hands, now seemed impotent. Rott looked up and studied the sprinkler heads that populated the ceiling of every room in the ship. Each nozzle was prepared to flood the room with Nutroxen a few days before the ship landed. That way, the re-instantiated crew and civilians would wake up to a clean, fungus free ship.

Should he engage the sprinklers or not? Rott decided against it, knowing that Bennish wouldn't allow him to take the easy way out. Oh well, guess it's time for a little hard labor.

Rott headed to the nearest storage cell, got down on his knees, and sprayed some Nutroxen around a cable's steel joint collar. He then proceeded to wipe the fungus off. Look at it all, he thought. What is going on here? First the P.O.T.U.s and now this! Well, he knew he was innocent, and he was angered that Mac had suspected him right away without even thinking that someone else could've been at fault. That really pissed him off. Now that he thought of it, he had never really liked Mac, he was always joking and smiling; you can't trust people like that, or Van Lank for that matter. He was always the friend to everyone, enemy of no one. Or was that an act too? Maybe they had it out for him. Maybe he was even being set up! Those bastards! Well I'm sure Bennish has it in for me, maybe he bled the P.O.T.U.s so he could blame me or, well, maybe it was one of the grounds crew. Damn, there's no way of knowing. And worst of all no way to clear my name. Screw 'em. Screw 'em all.

Rott angrily returned to the job at hand. He'd clean all the joints and control panels then come back later with additional supplies and do a more thorough job. It would be exhausting, tedious work but Rott was no stranger to menial labor.

Immediately after graduating high school, Rott decided to see the world; problem was, he didn't have any money to do it. But then a friend in the Nebraska National Guard asked if he'd like to accompany him, on Uncle Sam's dime, on a flight to Fairbanks, Alaska. The friend had to report to Fort Wainwright, but Rott could look around for a summer job and use any money he earned to get to Russia then work his way to Europe. Rott didn't have to think twice. He packed up and left home early the next morning, while his mother was sleeping off another drinking binge.

The cargo hold of the plane was cold and the constant buzz of the engines gave him an earache, but once Rott stepped onto Alaskan soil he felt he had accomplished something truly important for the first time. He had escaped the drudgery of his former life, which he intended to shed like a snake's skin.

A local hostel provided refuge for the night, where he had a fitful sleep bestowed upon him by the cockroaches and bedbugs. The next morning, Rott eagerly jumped on the bus that lumbered the three hundred odd miles to King Salmon, where he then hitched a ride to take him fifteen miles further south, to the town of Naknek. And it was there, at a small salmon cannery, that he learned the meaning of the phrase: 'a hard-day's night'.

In Alaska (before Earth's destruction), during the months from May to October, canneries hired temporary workers to help handle the fishing and processing of the five species of natural, wild salmon (king, red, coho, chum and pink) which thrived in the cold, clear waters. People from all over the world would congregate in the major fishing areas like moths to a lamp, not because they relished the prospect of the experience but because it provided decent wages for half a year's labor.

Rott's crew was a string mix: Japanese who were full-time employees that only handled the fish eggs and management (Rott never got along with them); Filipinos who were migrant workers that made the trip every year after their seasonal vegetable picking jobs in California ended (they played cribbage for $1 per point and laughed at the rest of the crew); a few guys that were down on their luck or running from the law (one man was arrested on an out-of-state warrant after he got into a fight with one of the Filipinos); and the young kids attracted by the quick buck.

But the money didn't come as quickly, or as easily, as they hoped. Each day was as monotonous as the previous one and as boring as the next. For Rott, the day began at 7:00am, when he'd report to the 'slime line' in the processing plant. For sixteen hours he'd have to check (by hand, mind you) the 10,000 pounds of fish that was gutted and de-finned by the loud, stinking machine to his left. Then at 11:00pm he'd sit down for his late dinner/early breakfast: a bowl of fish stew and a few pints of the local bar's warm, soapy brew. At 1:00am, he'd make the long walk back to the low, communal bunker and strive to grab a few hours rest.

Rott found sleeping difficult as the sun never really set; there was perpetual sunlight from 10:00pm until early morning. So he'd toss and turn before rising at 6:30am and starting the whole process all over again. Lather, rinse, repeat. Seven days per week. The constant sleep deprivation, coupled with the strange hours and back breaking labor, put the workers on edge and left a feeling of tension in the air; not the best climate for forging lasting friendships.

But Rott's nature neither attracted nor nurtured any type of true companionship anyway and, when a familiar face would appear before him, he'd nod his usual nod and snort his usual snort. Then he'd look to the ground and avoid projecting anything that could be misconstrued as eye contact.

One late June morning, hoping to clear his head, Rott took a hike down the lone paved road that connected the cannery to a small, weather-beaten airstrip. A ring of trash (rusted cars, washing machines, etc.) defined the town's roughly circular boundary. And past this Iron Curtain was nothing but pure tundra. Rott once tried to walk the mile to reach the river, the banks of which were dotted by bushes and small trees; the only sign of green life as far as the eye could see. But slogging through the tundra was tough; it was like walking in eighteen inches of thick moss. Rott abandoned the idea and turned back after half a mile. That's when something happened that would have a profound effect on his future.

One of the cannery's outdoor generators was spewing a thick, choking ribbon of smoke and a few of the staff mechanics had gathered round. As Rott walked by he noticed a chink in one of the fuel lines near the gasoline tanks. He looked on with amusement as the engineers concerned themselves with the generator and neglected to work their way back towards the tanks. Rott, in as few words as possible, pointed out the problem. The men were embarrassed but grateful and invited him to a real breakfast: fried eggs, bacon, homefries, juice, and coffee. That would be a welcome change from the cold cereal he had become accustomed to eating in his bunker. Rott's stomach growled at the prospect of consuming breakfast as he once knew it back in Nebraska. He eagerly accepted.

The men were friendly and easy to chum with. And though Rott listened much more than he spoke, he enjoyed their banter about the mechanical problems they encountered and their imaginative, if not creative, repairs they had to make here, in a forgotten place void of spare parts.

And the chance meeting snowballed into a job with the engineering crew. Rott soon found himself plowing through old 'fix-it-yourself' manuals, feeding his newly developed interest in mechanical engineering. And when his cannery stint was over, one of his new buddies, whose uncle was a professor at the University of Alaska Fairbanks, made a phone call and Rott was able to transition directly into the University's maintenance staff. A year later, Rott was one of the most promising students to ever step through its doors.

And now here he was, fourteen years removed from the cannery, down on his hands and knees and scrubbing a power cell to remove aspergillus, penicillium and fusarium; uncontrollable fungal growth that had only taken a day to blanket the cavernous room. It didn't make sense.

The hairs on the back of Rott's neck suddenly stood on end. He turned his head quickly towards the door. His subconscious mind had registered the threat of danger, as a housefly will anticipate the deadly thwack of a flyswatter. Bennish was standing in the doorway; his right hand rested lovingly on the butt of his sidearm. For a second, Bennish swayed on his feet, appearing to be unsteady. He swallowed hard and grimaced, as if his throat was hurting. But Rott couldn't know that it was Bennish's hard palate that was sore, stinging from the fix that was injected into it just minutes ago. Bennish steadied himself, smiled, and softly said, "Well, well, well. I finally found you." Bennish's squinting eyes examined the condition of the room. "And what do we have here?"

Rott thought Bennish looked like a Nazi general inhaling the scent of another town to conquer.

"I ordered you to manually check every power source; not the storage units," said Bennish threateningly.

Rott cleared his throat. "Don't go blaming me for this."

"Oh, I'll get to that. But first, why are you here and not checking the power sources?"

"You know as well as I do that fungus can get under protective coatings and oxidize copper cables. I wanted to make sure that power we generated was being saved properly. I wanted to be on top of things."

"On top of things?" screamed Bennish. "I know with fungus this advanced you didn't do what you were supposed to do to prevent this!" Bennish charged towards Rott, stopping right in front of him, standing over him like a lion over a felled deer.

Rott's brain instantly weighed and examined his options: fight, flight, or talk his way out. Bennish was still the captain but was acting less and less like a leader lately. But Rott decided that now, with no witnesses present, he'd be better off placating Bennish. It killed him to do what he did next. He cowered like a child expecting the slap. He spoke quickly, the words tumbling over each other. "I don't understand this. I ran ethylene oxide and methyl chloride gas through this area just three days ago. It should've killed all microbes."

Bennish turned and walked towards the room's environmental control pad. "You know as well as I do that the civilians, and us for that matter, brought new microbes on this ship the second we boarded." Bennish started swiping commands on the pad.

"I know that, but it doesn't make sense. Why is this room the only one infested?"

"Because, you stupid bastard," Bennish was now pointing towards some figures on the pad. "You had the humidity in this room set to seventy-five percent. You turned this room into a fucking petri dish. This stuff probably grew like weeds overnight. You stupid son-of-a-bitch."

Rott jumped up and ran towards the pad. He looked at its display with wide-eyed disbelief and fear of what was to come, like a child approaching its first visit with a mall Santa Claus. "I don't have the access code to the settings. You do. You locked them down!"

"I locked them down the day before launch. You were supposed to have them right by then."

"Then I don't understand this. I know I had it set right," stammered Rott. Dammit, he thought. You gotta be more careful. Don't give Bennish any more reasons to bust your balls.

Bennish looked at Rott with condemnation in his eyes. His inner judge deemed Rott guilty, decided on a sentence, and would mete out the punishment in due time. "You wouldn't be shirking any other duties, would you, Rottweiler?"

"No. Of course not!"

"Good," Bennish stood nose to nose with Rott. So close, in fact, that when Bennish breathed out of his nose, Rott could feel moisture forming on his upper lip. "So you're going to finish up here then check those power sources.

And then we won't have to worry about any more outages, right?"

"Right," Rott said through gritted teeth.

Bennish headed for the door. "Nice seeing you again, Rott. We really should see each other more often, seeing there's so little time left for us to be together."

Now what did that mean? I'm going to have to watch my back, and if Bennish is thinking of taking me out, I'll have to off him first. I'd be doing the New World a favor. Rott thought of the mission; of the New World, and how they'd be polluting it with people like Bennish and God knows how many more like him in stasis. Maybe the mission shouldn't succeed. Maybe The Chrysander was right after all.

14.
SUSPICIOUS MINDS

The flashing red photos on the monitor created little red pinpoints of light in Sandra's unblinking eyes as she furiously entered commands into her keyboard. Bennish was standing to her left, his right hand resting on the grip of his sidearm, his security blanket during times of stress, as he stared at the display. It read:

STRANDS INSTANTIATED:	5,052
CORRUPTED:	243
VIABLE:	4,809

"Well, it wasn't the power outage that did this," said Sandra. She had made a beeline to the Strand Data Room as soon as the power outage occurred. When she entered and saw that corruptions had increased more than tenfold since her last check, she immediately initiated a host of diagnostic utilities. She had been studying the preliminary results when Bennish walked in.

"Hapgood-"

"I'm on it, Captain. Should have results any second."

Bennish stared at the screen and said, "Jesus Christ! What a clusterfuck. So what is it?"

"I should know soon."

"Is it a problem with how you stranded them?"

"No, it's something else," said Sandra softly as she was preoccupied with the lines of diagnostic results that were streaming across her monitor.

"The mission will be aborted by the time you find out!"

"Let me figure this out by the numbers. Okay? Sir?"

"What about the strands that are corrupted, can you rebuild them?"

"No. For some reason their data's been chewed apart. There's no way of putting them back together in any coherent fashion." Sandra looked at Bennish to see if he understood. The look on his face wasn't promising so she continued, "It would be like putting your lunch back together after you've already eaten it."

"Yeah, I get it. Then you better find out what's causing it," said Bennish impatiently.

An alert popped up on the wall monitor stating that one of Sandra's utilities had finished its scan. Sandra explained the results. "Okay. So we know that it wasn't some rogue program or virus that was running in the background causing corruption. Now let's see what the next utility tells us."

"What's that one going to be looking for?"

"It's a deep hardware scan. Checking all the storage media; looking for the smallest deviation from what I specified."

"Now wait a minute. Aren't these systems designed so that even if one drive goes bad the data's been redundantly spread across multiple ones? I thought if data went bad you could always recover it."

Sandra let out a sigh as she shook her head. Did Bennish read any of the white papers she had drafted for his signature, where he was supposed to have acknowledged his review and understanding of the strand data system? She couldn't help but let a bit of sarcasm escape with her next statement. "If you remember reading the data system overview, you'd remember that human genome and memory mapping eats up a tremendous amount of storage space. And storage technology hasn't advanced enough to keep up. There aren't any backups or redundant anything. The precious space that is remaining, the space that would've been utilized if I had had a chance to strand a few more people, is being used by the system to duplicate bits of data that it thinks is corrupt or about to become corrupt. In theory, anyway."

"You can't add more data storage somehow?"

Sandra rolled her eyes. She spoke with controlled anger. "Every available resource is devoted to the strands." But her self-control left her for a second. Sandra pointed to the history computer next to her. "For God's sake, we're keeping the history of the world on its own computer. We couldn't cram its data anyplace else!"

Bennish wanted to say something, anything to put Sandra in her place for her lack of respect, but he couldn't think of anything to say that wouldn't expose his lack of knowledge even more than he already had.

A few seconds passed, then another alert popped up on the monitor. Sandra leaned forward to study the results intently, then leaned back in her chair. Bennish stared at her expectantly. "Well, don't just sit there! What does that goddamn gibberish mean?"

"It means that the storage media is fine, no defects found."

"So what does that tell us? I thought you were going to figure this out?"

"There's one more test result I'm waiting for. When I came in here and noticed there was more corruption than last night, I had a thought for updating a utility I had created when I first developed the stranding process. We used it in the early days of our lab, before we had these supercomputers to work on. I rewrote it so it would work with this system. It checks the spatial relationship of the corrupt data and the previously intact data. Basically, it tries to find how the data went wrong: application error, intentional deletion, etc. It's crude and slow but it might work."

"How slow is slow?"

"Until its finished." Sandra swiped a few keystrokes. A progress bar appeared on the monitor. The utility was almost finished. "Shouldn't be much longer."

Bennish stared at the monitor, feeling useless but wanting to say something that showed he was in control and not a subordinate. "This better work."

Sandra ignored the remark. She put her hand to her mouth and worried at a fingernail.

When the utility popped up its alert box, both Bennish and Sandra leaned forward in unison. Sandra's eyes were quickly scanning the results. Once they stopped, and her brain registered what she had read, she felt weak, nauseous, like the relative in a hospital waiting room hearing the grim prognosis from the surgeon.

Sandra swallowed so hard that Bennish immediately turned to her. "So what's going on here?"

Sandra slowly turned her head to Bennish. Her own mouth spoke the words, yet her brain couldn't believe she was saying them. "There's been system penetration, the corruption is intentional-"

Bennish exploded. "I knew we should've never let the ground crew techs work on these computers without better security measures-"

"You don't understand, sir."

Sandra tried to say the next sentence but she choked. Her throat had become unusually dry, as if the horrific news she was about to expose had sucked up all moisture from her tongue and throat. She gathered some saliva in her mouth and swallowed. Never in a million years did she ever dream it would come to this. She would never forget this room, this chair, the green and red icons flashing on the monitor, Bennish staring at her expectantly. If she lived to be a thousand, this moment's memory would be as fresh as today. She looked Bennish straight in the eye and said, "Someone on this ship is deleting strands."

Bennish's fingers wrapped around his sidearm tighter, like a boa constrictor squeezing the last ounce of life from a field mouse. "Who is it? Who has access?"

Sandra shook her head. "I don't know...there's no way of telling. There's over five thousand rooms on this ship to house everyone once we land. Each one has a computer and they're all networked."

"Turn off all access. Now."

"Can't. They're acting together as a supercomputer to store and process the strands."

"You're telling me you can't secure the data you're responsible for? Was this your design, Hapgood?"

"Captain," said Sandra, still light-headed from her painful discovery. "The computers were designed to separate once everyone was re-instantiated. Remember, we rushed to build this ship and everything in it. But we did incorporate revolving security codes. That's why whoever did this couldn't corrupt all the strands at once. But that's the extent of our security. We didn't think we'd have to protect ourselves against sabotage attempts committed by our fellow crewmembers, the same ones chosen to save humanity!"

"Well, we do," said Bennish testily. "And we have five thousand access sites. And someone under my command is using them to fuck with me."

"I don't believe it, I just don't believe it. Maybe there's a stowaway. Someone we missed-"

"Stowaway my ass. This ship was scanned nightly since the day it was built," said Bennish. His eyes lit up. "Would the person that's doing this know that we know? Know that you found it's intentional and not just data corruption?"

"No," said Sandra. "I programmed that last utility myself. No one would know that we discovered the system breech, unless we told them."

"Good. We're going to find who's doing this and I'm going to shoot the bastard right between the eyes."

"I just had a thought," said Sandra. "If someone is under The Chrysander's control, and doing this to ruin the mission, how could they guarantee they'd corrupt all of the strands before they were found out?"

Bennish shook his head. "What are you talking about?"

"If someone wanted to ruin the mission, why take a chance on ruining a few strands at a time, why not ruin everything about the mission?" Sandra looked hard at Bennish, hoping he could figure out what, to her, was the next logical step they would need to take. When Bennish didn't reply, she prompted him. "We have to check one more thing."

"What's that?"

"The re-instantiation procedure."

Bennish nodded his head slowly. "What do you want me to do?"

"I need you to order Recombinant Lab One to be brought online," Sandra said firmly. "We need to bring a strand back to life."

* * *

"We're ready for strand re-instantiation, Captain."

Sandra Hapgood was sitting in the Strand Data Room, her seat twisted to face one of the ten monitors on the left hand wall. It was displaying the interior of Recombinant Lab One. The camera was focused on the twelve foot tall by four foot wide steel cylinder that stood in the center of the room. It was in this tube that water, minerals and amino acids would be bombarded by electrical and chemical altering agents. The various molecules of this primordial soup would bind with each other in a predetermined way, guided by the strand data of the individual that was being re-instantiated. Within about two minutes the stranded subject would be, once again, a living, breathing human being, with all faculties and memories restored.

"Initiate re-instantiation," ordered Bennish.

Earlier, when Sandra had suggested a test of the re-instantiation process, she experienced, what she thought now, was a revelation. She convinced Bennish the subject they picked should be one with an easy-going disposition, as he would have to immediately endure a second, possibly risky, stranding process. Bennish inquired if Sandra remembered a subject that would fit the profile and she answered in the affirmative. She seemed to remember one subject named Wayne Evans, a docile, middle-aged man who had followed her orders without question. Sandra knew that Bennish would be most receptive to this type of an individual.

In reality, Wayne Evans was Sergeant Wayne Bailey, an undercover agent for Homeland Security. She had been introduced to Wayne years ago at a SuperBowl party. Once the re-instantiation was complete, Sandra planned to take Wayne into the Strand Extraction Lab and bring him up to speed regarding the deletion of the strands and her concerns regarding Bennish's recent behavior. She would then report to Bennish that the strand sampler was malfunctioning and Wayne would need to spend the night with the crew. Wayne was slim of build and only stood about five feet seven, but he was a master martial artist and could easily overpower or disarm any male crewmember if the need arose. Bennish had agreed to Sandra's recommendation and stated he would go inform the crew.

Once the captain had left Sandra alone in the Strand Data Room, she immediately checked the status of Evelyn's strand. She was relieved to see its integrity was one hundred percent. Sandra confirmed that the revolving security codes were in place and then she exited the room.

She made a beeline to the Planet Assessment Room, where she found Van Lank leaning back in his chair, sipping a glass of iced tea. He was surrounded by a number of monitors, each of them displaying a different planet and its general fitness for human life. Graphical data detailing temperature, atmospheric composition, H2O availability, and chemical composition scrolled across the screens. Van Lank turned and smiled broadly when he realized Sandra had entered.

"Okay, what's your guess?"

"What?" said Sandra, pre-occupied.

"The picture in my room, the watercolor. Are you going to guess what beach it is?"

"Ryan, I have something more important-"

But Van Lank was in a playful mood. Ever since Sandra had returned from successfully saving Mac, he was almost giddy in Sandra's presence. "Come on, lighten up. Just make a guess."

"The Maldives Islands. Listen, Ryan-"

"No, not the Mald-"

Sandra literally stomped her foot. "Ryan! Listen to me. We have major problems!" Tears welled up in her eyes.

Van Lank immediately shot out of his chair and reached out to Sandra. He guided her gently into his seat and handed her his glass of tea. Sandra took it in both hands and drank deeply from it while Van Lank stroked her hair. Sandra drained the glass and placed it on the desk. "You're not going to believe this," she said in a soft voice.

Van Lank pulled another chair up and sat in it, then leaned forward and grabbed Sandra's hands in his. "Try me."

Sandra wiped her tears with the back of her hand. She took a deep breath and launched into her story. She explained everything that happened with Bennish in the Strand Data Room, right down to the smallest detail. When she finished, Van Lank slowly stood up and started pacing the room.

"You're right. I can't believe it." Van lank shook his head. "Someone on this ship, one of us, is deleting strands? I just can't believe it."

"It's true."

"What are we going to do? How can we catch whomever it is, or at least keep the strands safe?"

"Well, we're going to have help. I'm going to re-instantiate a Homeland Security agent, but Bennish thinks it's going to be just some meek individual."

"That's brilliant."

"And I had another thought as I came over here." Sandra's voice became stronger and determination showed in her face. "If I can rig it so strand data can only be accessed from the Strand Data Room, could you set up some sort of security system in there?"

Van Lank bit his lip. "I'd have to cannibalize some equipment to do that. And the only cameras that are available is the one you use to take pictures of the stranded civilians and the ones that monitor the recombinant labs."

"You'd never get those out; they're built into the cylinders steel liners. It'll have to be the one in the Strand Extraction Lab."

"That one's no good. It's a fixed focal length camera and, anyway, I'd have to hack into the wall. It would be noticeable as hell. No, I need to build something from parts the others won't notice missing." Van Lank changed gears. "You're not going to tell anyone else about this Bailey guy, not even Bennish, right?"

"Are you kidding? Especially Bennish."

Van Lank nodded his head slowly in agreement. "Good. So is he going to order the re-instantiation?"

"Yes. So be prepared and keep your eyes peeled. If you see anything out of the ordinary, anything suspicious at all, make note of it and let me know later when no one's around."

Bennish's voice suddenly emanated from the wall speaker. "Van Lank and Minami, report to Recombinant Lab One on the double."

Van Lank smiled meekly at Sandra. "Duty calls." He put his hand out and Sandra took it. Van Lank helped her to her feet. They shared a quick kiss. "Don't worry, Sandra. We'll figure this out. Together." They kissed again and exited the Planet Assessment Room.

And now, as Sandra sat in the Strand Data Room staring at the live video feed from Recombinant Lab One, she flipped the switch that would transfer Wayne Bailey's strand data, along with a flow of water, mineral and protein components, into the recombinant lab's re-instantiation cylinder. Now we wait, thought Sandra, to see if the re-instantiation proves successful or if the perpetrator of the corrupted strands has also sabotaged the ability to bring them back to life.

15.
HUMANOID

The re-instantiation cylinder's glass window, though only about the size of a hardcover book, provided an almost hypnotic display of the strand rebuilding process. The swirling proteins and chemicals, in conjunction with the enzymes, catalysts, and electrical pulses, reminded Van Lank of New Year's Eve, for it looked like a family of confetti, with party popper guests, was hosting their own little celebratory party inside the steel cylinder. Another fifteen seconds, thought Van Lank, and the process will be over. Another ten seconds for the cylinder to cool down and the steam to clear, then it will automatically unlock its access door and Wayne Bailey will step out as if returning from a walk in the park. Then I'll hand him this robe and I'll quickly brief Bailey about the situation, to ensure he plays the docile subject to the hilt. If I talk quickly and low enough, even Mineko won't hear me.

Van Lank turned and smiled at Mineko, who was standing just inside the entranceway, about thirty feet from the cylinder. The plain, white room was circular in shape and the cylinder stood exactly in the middle, like the hub of a wheel. The ceiling was covered with a series of color coded pipes and conduits that carried the water and other ingredients. The walls were lined with storage cabinets, on top of which sat numerous computers and servers.

It was the ungodly, inhuman scream that caused Van Lank to quickly turn back to the cylinder.

The swirling confetti had stopped, and as Mineko and Van Lank each took a tentative step towards the cylinder, a red, raw, bloody, three-fingered hand pressed up against the inside of the glass.

Mineko gasped audibly. "My God, what is that?"

"I don't know," said Van Lank as he took another, shorter step forward. "Maybe I better engage the access door lock-"

The steel door swung open with such force that it almost tore itself from its hinges. A burst of super heated steam bellowed into the room. And what stepped out from behind the white cloud was a being that only exists in nightmares.

It stood about eight feet tall. Its feet were gnarled yet paw like, and they twitched uncontrollably. Long curved 'toenails' tapped the floor independently of each other, ten Morse code operators transmitting at once. The legs were tri-jointed, and the tendons and ligaments were outside of the skin, which was mottled with patches of pigmented human epidermis, and large areas of thick, blood soaked fur. The arms were long and thickly muscled, with hands the size of bananas. The nails resembled paring knives, and looked about as sharp. The torso was an amalgam of misshapen ribs, cartilage, and inflating and deflating 'bags' which must have been external lungs. The head had two marble-sized eyes, the only thing it shared with a normal human. The brain was visible through its malformed skull, which was riddled with holes. The gills on the neck explained the absence of the nose, and they were inhaling and exhaling laboriously. A bloody mist emanated from them rhythmically. The mouth was large, and the bleeding, puss-pocketed gums were studded with two rows of overlapping, shark-like teeth.

Wayne Bailey, or what was once Wayne Bailey before his re-instantiation went horribly wrong, glanced around the room like a cornered, wild animal. It looked up at the bright lights and, even though opaque, secondary eyelids covered the pupils, it shielded its eyes with its arms. Then this humanoid, this perverse offspring of Mother Nature and man's genetic fiddling, emitted an ear-piercing, mournful wail.

Van Lank stood stock-still, his knees were bent and his arms were away from his body. He looked like he was balancing on a surfboard with the white robe hanging from his right hand. "Mineko, back out as slowly as possible." Van Lank's mouth hardly moved. Mineko took the opportunity to slide her feet back across the smooth, ceramic tiles while the humanoid was still cowering under the lights. Once her left foot felt the indentation of the door track, she twisted and deftly exited the room.

Just as quickly, Bennish appeared in the doorway. He immediately turned his body forty-five degrees to the humanoid and brought his gun up in a standard two-handed grip. "Stand aside, Van Lank, you're in my line of fire."

Bennish knew he only had ten seconds to get a shot off, any longer than that and his raised arms would start to waver, affecting his aim.

Van Lank leaned steeply to his right, and as Bennish started to squeeze the trigger, Sandra's voice emanated from the intercom speaker. "No! Pierce the hull and you'll kill us all!"

Bennish lowered the gun. "Shit." Though Bennish was sure he would hit the human monstrosity, the muzzle velocity of his 124 grain bullets would result in a 'through and through' wound, and there would be a chance, granted a very small chance, of compromising the hull.

The combination of Sandra's warning and Bennish's epithet, caused the humanoid to forget about the ceiling lights and scan the room, like a tiger eyeing the savannah for game. Its eyes settled on Van Lank. It bared its teeth, emitted a low growl, and leaped toward him.

* * *

When Sandra Hapgood saw the deformed hand strike the recombinant cylinder's window, she immediately knew something had gone horribly wrong. "Captain, Emergency in Recombinant Lab One!" she screamed into her microphone.

Since the humanoid broke the door open before she could override the locking mechanism, Sandra knew she had to find a way to neutralize the possible threat that it posed. A germ of an idea formed and she ran out of the Strand Data Room. She slipped as she tried to make a sharp turn, fell to the ground, and rolled back on her feet in one smooth motion.

The entrance to the Strand Extraction Lab was down the hall, forty feet away, thirty, twenty, ten. Sandra grabbed the doorframe to shift her momentum and she flung herself inside. She maneuvered around the partition and dove to the floor, sliding to a stop at the strand sampler gun. She pulled it out of its slot and disconnected the thick cable from its grip. There was still a strip of six, four-inch long Lexan tubes hanging out of the side of the sampler, like the ammunition belt of a machine gun, ready for loading. Sandra popped open the small access door that was located on the top rear of the sampler, where the hammer would be on a revolver. She reached in and released a retaining clip and jammed the door shut.

The intercom came alive. "Stand aside, Van Lank, you're in my line of fire."

That stupid bastard, thought Sandra. She stood up and yelled as she ran for the door. "No! Pierce the hull and you'll kill us all!"

Sandra ran faster than she had ever run before in her life, but towards what? By the time Sandra's stranding research had reached the small mammal stage, all possible re-instantiation errors had been fixed. The worse 'botched' subject she had ever seen recreated was probably a worm, which still looked normal, but its internal organs had not fully formed. But this thing! That three-fingered hand was at least twice as large as normal. Would the rest of its anatomy match a human's close enough so that it could be killed by normal means? She hoped her makeshift weapon would work.

Mineko was crouching beside Recombinant Lab One's entrance, carefully peeking into the room. The sound of

Sandra's footsteps telegraphed her approach and Mineko vaulted to her feet and grabbed Sandra by her shoulders.

"It's horrible!" cried Mineko, her face a mask of terror, as she shook Sandra uncontrollably. If just looking at the humanoid has caused this much fear in Mineko, thought Sandra, then I better prepare myself now, for if I hesitate for just one second once I enter the lab and lay eyes on it, it could be fatal for Van Lank.

"I know," said Sandra firmly, "I have to stop it." She shook herself free from Mineko and leaped into the room. Within a millisecond, her mind had taken in and processed the scene before her.

Bennish was standing off to the left, holding his pistol before him like a cross, as if warding off a vampire. The white robe Van Lank had been holding was near the cylinder, torn to threads. He must have tossed it at the humanoid as it charged towards him and, luckily, it made for the robe like a bull to a matador's red muleta. But the ruse only delayed the inevitable, as the humanoid was now standing above Van Lank, who cowered on the floor against one of the cabinets. Too bad he didn't climb into one, thought Sandra. But then she dismissed the idea. The humanoid was huge, and now, as she processed the image of this perversion of man for the first time, she realized that he'd tear the doors off these cabinets as easily as a child could tear the wings off a fly.

Blood was pouring from Van Lank's left ear, or where his ear used to be. Sandra noticed the blood on the humanoid's right hand. He must've swiped at Van Lank's head and tore the ear clean off. The humanoid would now go in for the kill. It was time to act.

Sandra raised the strand sampler gun in a two handed grip. She prayed that the tool that would save humankind would save Van Lank as well. Since the sampler gun had enough internal force to instantly pierce a human's skull with its Lexan tubes, she believed that by taking out the retaining clip, the tubes would shoot out of the sampler as a bullet leaves a gun. She had never tried or tested this before. Why would she have?

The humanoid was standing at a right angle to her, about thirty feet away. She only had a side profile to shoot at; a poor target. Since the sampler gun did not have sights or any type of aiming mechanism on it, she took her best guess and pulled the trigger.

'Thrupft'

The first tube shot across the room and over the humanoid's head. It struck the wall with a loud 'crack' and bounced to the floor. Sandra didn't see any of this, for as soon as she fired the first shot, she adjusted her aim and prepared for the second. The humanoid, hearing the tube hit the wall, had turned towards it, away from Van Lank. Sandra now had the full, backside profile of it as a target. She took a bit more time to aim this time and squeezed the trigger again.

'Thrupft'

The wall behind the humanoid splattered with blood and tissue as the tube tore a strip of flesh off the right shoulder. It howled in pain, turned, and shook its head violently. It set its eyes on Sandra.

'Thrupft'

The third tube exited the sampler and lodged in the humanoid's stomach. Blood began to pour out of the tube in a steady stream, like maple sap through a spile. The humanoid faltered for a second then started running at Sandra, who bravely stood her ground, willing the next few shots to finally hit a crucial organ or artery.

'Thrupft'

'Thrupft'

The fourth and fifth shots both shattered the sternum and entered the chest cavity, injuries that would prove fatal to a human with normal anatomy. Yet the humanoid, roaring like a wounded lion, not only stayed upright but was now charging even faster towards Sandra. What the hell, she thought, only one shot left. It has to be a headshot. I can't afford to miss; I have to wait until he's right upon me!

The events of the next few seconds seemed to happen in slow motion. As the humanoid approached Sandra and she aimed the sampler between its eyes, the remnants of human intelligence in its brain recognized that the thing that had placed holes in its body was now about to do the same to its head. It slid to a stop and swiped at the sampler, right as Sandra began to pull the trigger. Too late, Sandra realized the reach of the humanoid's hand was much longer than she had estimated. Before getting the shot off, she had to fall backwards to avoid having her face raked by the razor sharp nails. Sandra was now flat on her back, watching the humanoid raise its hand to swipe yet again, to rip her open from neck to groin.

Dejectedly, Sandra realized she would not be able to raise the sampler in time to hit anything further up the humanoid's body than its leg, maybe its stomach. For some reason, at this moment when all seemed lost and death was imminent, all Sandra could think of as she saw the knife-like nails come down towards her was this: I'm a camper facing the ransacking bear, the sadistic lion tamer getting his due.

When Sandra saw the cabinet door whack the mammal in the back of its head, she realized that Van Lank must've lifted it off its hinges and flung it like a Frisbee across the room. The humanoid, more angered than hurt, turned his head towards Van Lank. This provided Sandra with her one, her only, chance.

In high school, Sandra had hoped to become a cheer-leader, and she was eagerly accepted after the first tryout. She was naturally flexible with a good sense of balance and her coach choreographed routines explicitly to show-case Sandra's acrobatic capabilities. Two years in a row, she and her fellow cheerleaders made the trip to Orlando and won the U.S. Open Championship. But, unlike most of her fellow cheerleaders (and most high school athletes), once Sandra entered the working world, she continued to keep her body in peak physical condition. And after she joined NASA, it was a requirement. Granted, she hadn't worked out much during the past year, but all she needed was for her body to perform one move, one acrobatic trick that, though she hadn't practiced it in months, was hopefully nestled deeply in her 'muscle memory'.

As the humanoid turned its head towards Van Lank and emitted its blood-curdling scream, Sandra drew her legs into her chest. She then placed her hands against the floor near her ears and, while thrusting her legs upward and outwards, she pushed off the floor with her hands and shoulders. Though the sampler in her right hand cost her a bit of momentum, her body lifted into the air. She arched her back and used her abdominal muscles to pull her torso into an upright position as her feet landed on the floor. In one second, Sandra went from lying flat on her back to an upright squatting position, thanks to a perfectly executed kip-up.

Sandra's eyes zeroed in on her next and final target. She leaped up and, while still in midair, pressed the sampler's muzzle under the humanoid's chin and pulled the trigger.

'Thrupft'

The Lexan tube easily tore through the mylohyoid muscle, tongue, hard palate, and nasal cavity. It then broke through the ethmoid bone and entered the brain where, due to its bouncing around inside the skull, it ground the brain into hamburger. The Lexan tube, after expending its energy, happened to find one of the holes in the humanoid's skull and, its job finished, dropped harmlessly to the floor.

The humanoid's arms and legs, now under orders from a leaderless central nervous system, shook involuntarily. Its eyes rolled back in its head and it crashed face first onto the floor like a glass-jawed boxer.

Sandra Hapgood stood over the maimed and mangled mass of flesh and bone; flesh and bone of what once was a vibrant, normal human being named Wayne Bailey. Sandra shifted her gaze to the re-instantiation cylinder, the womb from which this monstrosity had been borne, the womb that was decreed to give birth to humankind on a New World. She wondered if she or any other crewmember would live to see it.

PART 3

THE END OF THE BEGINNING

16.
GUILT BY ASSOCIATION

"I can't believe it," said Sandra shaking her head. "I just can't believe it."

"I knew who it was all along," said Bennish proudly. "Damn I sure did."

Sandra and Bennish were standing in the Medical Clinic. An unconscious Van Lank rested peacefully on a bed to their right. The humanoid, now headless, was thrown haphazardly on another bed to their left.

"What are you going to do? Interrogate? If this was done because of some twisted belief in The Chrysander's preaching, then interrogation might reveal what else on this ship has been compromised. But, if this behavior was the result of brainwashing, then interrogation will be useless. A brainwashed person won't even know what they've been doing."

Bennish slammed his fist on the equipment bench. "There has to be a way to find out."

Sandra was deep in thought. "Well, there is a way, but-"

155

"How?"

"You strand a person then test their brain matter for biochemical manipulation or altered synaptic structure."

"That's perfect," said Bennish excitedly. "If we find evidence of brain washing, we re-instantiate them once we settle the New World. But if we find the sabotage was intentional, we re-instantiate immediately and interrogate the living shit-"

Sandra, who had been shaking her head while Bennish was speaking, interrupted him. "It doesn't work like that, Captain. Once you take the brain matter and test it, it wipes out the tapped cortex. The re-instantiated person would have basic motor functions and baseline intelligence. All memories would be lost."

Bennish slammed the bench again. "Goddammit!" He had a crushing, mind-numbing headache. He needed a fix desperately.

"Are you all right?" queried Sandra.

"I'll be fine," said Bennish as he stood up ram-rod straight. "I have to go." Bennish made for the door.

"Captain, what are you going to do?"

"You'll see," said Bennish with an evil smile. "Let's just say your strands are going to be safe." Bennish waved a hand at the humanoid. "And we won't have any more of these friggin' Frankensteins running around."

Bennish exited the room as Sandra turned towards Van Lank.

* * *

Immediately after Sandra had killed the humanoid, Mineko and Bennish helped her carry Van Lank to his current position where Sandra administered a fast acting anesthetic. She then thanked the others for their assistance and, as soon as they left, she used multi-angled facial photos from Van Lank's dossier to create a silicon polymer ear in the 3D printer.

Once Sandra placed the ear in position on Van Lank's head, she used an ultrasound probe to seal it in place. By this time, Bennish had returned from Recombinant Lab One, where he took samples of the water, amino acids, vitamins, and minerals that were used in Wayne Bailey's re-instantiation. He placed the vials on the bench. "Did you check that monster yet?"

"I just finished with Ryan's ear. Let's test the humanoid right now."

Sandra proceeded to the end of the bench, where the humanoid's head rested on a steel tray. She placed a few grams of brain matter into a perforated glass sphere and placed it into a small diagnostic machine. Almost immediately, a stream of scrolling letters representing DNA code and amino acid structure appeared on its associated monitor. Sandra stared intently at the hundreds of letters that flashed by every few seconds.

"I don't know how you make heads or tails out of that crap."

"It's like reading music. Once you know the notes you can recognize the ones that don't belong." Sandra typed something into the keyboard and the scrolling data stopped. She turned to Bennish. "Wayne Bailey's strand data was fine," said Sandra as she slowly turned to stare at the vials that Bennish brought in.

"So some bastard contaminated the materials used to re-instantiate him."

"Let's not blame anyone until we test them." Sandra took some samples of the components that were contained in the vials and placed them into the gas chromatography/mass spectrometry instrument. Within a few seconds, the monitor displayed the results.

"Well, the water is pure hydrogen and oxygen, which makes sense because it's filtered right at the cylinder. Now, let's see about the other components," said Sandra as she read from the monitor. "Lysine, arginine, selenium, potassium...so far so good...wait a minute..."

"What is it?" asked Bennish excitedly.

"Quaternary ammonium chloride...phenol...sodium hypochlorite...and hydrogen peroxide. You gotta be kidding me."

"What? What do mean? What is it?"

"These are the ingredients of Nutroxen."

"You mean the disinfectant that Rott's using to kill fungus?"

"Yes," said Sandra solemnly. "One and the same. So someone's working both angles, deleting the strands and tainting the materials needed to bring them back."

"Someone my ass, it's Rott and I knew it," said Bennish as he rubbed his hands greedily, fantasizing about the punishment he would now be able to meter out.

"I can't believe it," said Sandra shaking her head. "I just can't believe it."

"I knew who it was all along," said Bennish proudly. "Damn I sure did."

And, as Bennish left the room after promising that the strands would now be safe, Sandra turned towards the bench and held it for support. She felt faint and nauseous.

Not because a trusted crewmember had been implicated in one of the most horrendous crimes ever committed against humankind, but because the person might be an unwitting perpetrator, a brainwash victim of The Chrysander, and she may have just signed his death warrant.

Sandra turned and looked at Van Lank as he slept peacefully. She went over to him and checked his vitals, which were normal. How she wanted to talk to him! But he'd wake in another thirty minutes or so, once the sedation wore off. Sandra grabbed the edges of the sheet and the thin blanket that covered Van Lank and pulled them up closer to his neck. She then kissed him lightly on the forward, took one last look around the clinic, whispered the word 'unbelievable', and exited the clinic.

Sandra proceeded to the Strand Data Room, glanced up at the green and red photos upon entering, then hurried to her seat. She was relieved to see that no further strands had been deleted since her last check. Of course not, she thought, the perpetrator (she refused to fully believe it was Rott) had been busy sabotaging other things.

Sandra sat deep in thought for a minute than began typing furiously on the keyboard. Her concentration did not waver for the next twenty minutes, when she finally sat back with a small sense of satisfaction on her face. After a few seconds, she reached for the history computer, rewound a bit, and played back the last entry. She watched a static, file photo of herself while her words played out. "Planet Earth subjected to total nuclear destruction. Survivors: none. Cause of event...man's will. Or lack of it."

Sandra engaged the record button and spoke from the heart. "Evelyn, Evelyn honey, I want you to know what's happening, what has happened here in case I can't tell you personally in the New World. Someone on this ship is deleting strands, messing with the ship, trying to prevent us from doing our duty. I'm doing what I can to protect the strands and yours especially. I've altered your strand's signature, so hopefully it can't be deleted easily. I know someday you'll hear this because I know we'll find who's doing this. I'll talk to you again soon."

Sandra stopped the recorder and checked the time. Ryan will be awake any minute now, she thought. She headed toward the exit in haste.

When she returned to the Medical Clinic, Van lank was moving fitfully under the sheet, like a man having a nightmare. Sandra shook him gently while whispering softly in his ear. "It's all right. Everything's all right now." Van Lank opened his eyes, shook his head like a dog coming in from the rain, and looked deeply into Sandra's eyes. She leaned in and, as they shared a passionate kiss, Van Lank pulled Sandra onto the stretcher with him.

Sandra squealed as she fell on top of Van Lank, but then her mouth searched for his again and they embraced tightly, their legs entwined. They separated just long enough to quickly undo the fasteners of their clothing. Within a minute, they were panting with hot lust, like wild animals in heat. And when Van Lank entered her she had to bite his shoulder to stifle a scream. For the next twenty minutes nothing else, nor anyone else, existed in the whole world.

"Wow, that felt good," said Van Lank as he fell back onto the stretcher.

"You deserved it after what you've been through," said Sandra, who was sitting up, straddling him.

"Maybe I should lose an ear more often. I wonder if Van Gogh had it as good as this!" Van Lank laughed heartily.

"I'll take that as a compliment." Sandra kissed Van Lank quickly on the lips.

"You realize we have to do this again before we go into stasis."

"Oh really? Why?"

"Well, we're supposed to populate a New World once we're re-instantiated, right?" Van Lank smiled slyly. "This will keep us in practice."

Sandra looked at Van Lank incredulously. "Are you really sure? You're ready for us to have a child together?"

"Of course I'm sure."

Sandra smiled broadly, leaned in, and planted a big kiss on Van Lank's lips. "I love you, Ryan."

"I love you too, Sandra," Van Lank propped himself on one elbow. "And I also want to thank you for saving my life earlier." Van Lank tipped an imaginary hat, and in his best John Wayne voice said, "That was good shooting today, pardner. Damn good shooting."

Sandra held her hand up and blew across the tip of her outstretched index finger, as a cowboy might blow across the muzzle of his still smoking gun. "Someone had to clean up this one horse town."

Van Lank laughed heartily. Sandra was pleased to see him truly happy. She cursed herself that she would have to ruin his mood with her news about the humanoid's origin. To Ryan, the monster was an aberration, an accident. He didn't yet know the level of treachery a fellow crewmember had reached. Sandra wanted to keep the good times rolling for him, at least for another second.

"Meghan's Bay," said Sandra firmly.

"What?"

"Meghan's Bay. You know, in St. Thomas." Sandra repeated. "The painting in your room. Is that it?"

"Oh," said Van Lank as he caught the reference. "No, not Meghan's Bay. Not Meghan's Bay," he repeated as his smile faded. Van Lank had sensed the change in Sandra. The party atmosphere was now over for him also. "So tell me, what the hell happened in the lab?"

"Tainted re-instantiation components. Someone's hitting us from both sides, the strands and the rebuilding process. Bennish thinks it Rott."

"Why?"

"We found Nutroxen in the mix."

Van Lank rubbed his face and pushed his hair back from his forehead. "Oh man…"

"I can't believe it either." A waterfall of words started to flow from Sandra's mouth as if she couldn't wait to share all of her thoughts with Van Lank. "I told Bennish that Rott may be brainwashed and I could strand Rott and check for cortex manipulation but he'd be a zombie after that and so maybe interrogation wouldn't tell us anything-"

Van Lank slid off the stretcher. "What's Bennish going to do about it?"

"I don't know, he said he'd take care of it."

"Rott's a dead man. You know that, right?"

"Yes, and I feel terrible. I found the Nutroxen."

"Don't blame yourself. Maybe Bennish is right. If Rott is doing this he's gunning to ruin the mission. We can't let our personal feelings interfere. How are the strands doing?"

"I'm still working on limiting their access to the data room. If I succeed, then all of us should just sit in that room together until its time for us to go into stasis."

Van Lank rubbed his hand through his hair. When he spoke he was exasperated. "If only we could, but we can't. We have power issues, a damaged thruster, programming to do. We can't all sit around jerkin' each other off."

"I know that, but what do we do?"

Van Lank spun around. "If Bennish takes care of Rott, and we have no further strand corruptions, then we're good as gold."

"But what if Rott's not the one doing this?"

Van Lank looked hard at Sandra. "Then we know it's one of five that is."

17.
FOOL'S ERRAND

Bennish squeezed the bridge of his nose between thumb and forefinger. His eyes were so tightly closed that his cheeks practically touched his forehead. He was bent over and wavering like a homeless man picking up a dime in the street. One hand was steadying himself against the door frame of his closet while the other hung on loosely to the transdermal device. Jesus, he thought, that felt good!

Bennish straightened himself up and clumsily placed the device on the top shelf. He rubbed his face and, like a deck hand walking stem to stern in heavy seas, he staggered towards the exit of his quarters.

By the time Bennish made it to the cockpit area, he had regained a semblance of composure. Mineko turned in her chair, placed the mask of subordination on her face and queried, "Orders, Captain?"

"All engines off. Exhaust vents closed. We need to make repairs."

Mineko swiped some commands into her console's keyboard.

"Engines shutting down, sir," said Mineko as she tracked some graphics on her monitor. "Exhaust vents closed in three, two, one. Now." The ship shook ever so slightly as the massive exhaust vent doors to the four thrusters sealed shut.

"Where's Rottweiler?"

"Last report, still cleaning the power cables."

Bennish grunted and engaged the intercom. "Rottweiler," he said gruffly.

After a pause, Rottweiler's voice rang clearly from the wall speaker. "What...yes, Captain?"

"I want you to suit up and enter the main thruster housing; through the inner access panel, not from outside. Mac says the power feed lines were damaged. Want to see if you can repair them."

"We're doing all right with the power generated from the other three mains, the power drop we had earlier was from the fungus," replied Rott.

Mineko noticed that Bennish was holding the butt of his sidearm so tightly that his knuckles were white. She looked up at Bennish's face. An angry vein near his temple was pulsing fast, swollen like a fireman's hose. Every time his Adam's apple bobbed up and down, he grimaced a bit as if he had strep throat. Mineko noticed his eyes were glassy and unfocused. She sniffed the air in a failed attempt to detect alcohol.

"We don't know if one of the other mains will fail. I want all four working perfectly, making power," growled Bennish.

"Maybe I should consult with Mac first, to see if I even have a chance of rerouting-"

"I already talked to Mac," Bennish's voice was now smooth as honey. "Just take some cyrolert cabling and synbestos cable shields with you."

Silence.

"Now, Rottweiler. While we're still young." Bennish laughed uncharacteristically.

"Okay," said Rott. "I'll notify you when I'm in the main."

"Great," said Bennish smiling. "Bennish out."

Bennish turned to Mineko. He was still smiling. But it was not one of humor; it was a smile that held a secret. "This should fix our problem."

"Our power problem?" offered Mineko.

"Our personnel problem," said Bennish menacingly.

* * *

"Captain, I'm at the access door," said Rott into his helmet's microphone.

"Roger that. We're opening it now," echoed Bennish's reply.

Rott was standing in front of one of the four, twelve feet round, three feet thick, doors. The engineers jokingly referred to the doors as 'the vaults' as they contained extremely complex locking mechanisms controlled exclusively from the cockpit. They couldn't afford some mischievous person in the New World sandpapering his fingertips then cracking the door open. Even though the engines were designed not to fire with the exhaust vent doors closed, if that safety feature failed, and an access door was open, a test fire of the main engines or an emergency launch would subject the interior of the *Prometheus* to a fountain of molten plasma, which would instantly incinerate all hundred floors and then exit the cockpit windows, like lava spewing from a volcano. For all intents and purposes, the *Prometheus* would become a thousand foot tall Roman Candle.

With the sound of a thunderclap, the door's bolts pulled back, the electronic motors engaged, and the door cracked open away from Rott, into the interior of the engine housing. This was the last 'failsafe' feature, though it had never been tested. If, by chance, the engines fired and the exhaust vents were closed, the pressure of the exhaust would, theoretically, slam the access doors shut. The power transfer lines and feedback units would be obliterated instantly but at least the ship would be saved.

Since Rott couldn't rely on a P.O.T.U. to maneuver in the engine housing, he was relying on his magnetic boots and their 'smart' function: when the boot sensed that a person's foot was bending to take a step, it would weaken its magnetic force then strengthen again once it 'felt' the heel and arch make contact again with a surface. A person had to walk with an exaggerated gait but the smart feature of the boots kept leg and ankle strain at a minimum. Rott stepped carefully through the space between the door and its frame, then placed one foot tentatively below the door's sill.

Though he was in a zero gravity environment, his eyes told him he would be walking 'down' the wall, and he found it disconcerting to walk straight down after passing through a doorway. But the boot stuck like glue and Rott confidently brought his other foot around to join the first.

The interior of the housing was dark as night. The small tear in the housing did not provide any light at all, not even a splattering of stars that would identify the tear's location. And the small amount of light coming through the door's opening behind Rott was negated by the helmet's polarized visor. Rott couldn't see anything; not even his white-gloved hand held in front of his face. He was blind. He was Mizaru, one of the three wise monkeys, eyes covered so as to see no evil. Well, there wasn't any evil here, thought Rott, except maybe for that bastard Bennish on the bridge. And, as if to banish the thought of Bennish, Rott engaged his helmet's omnispotlight, and the area was bathed in a cold, harsh light.

Main Thruster Four was about the size of a small apartment building, so it took Rott the better part of fifteen minutes to circumnavigate the inner side of the housing, until he came upon the tear in the ship's skin and the sheared power transfer cables. The cables terminated in junction boxes every few feet and Rott examined them closely. Son-of-a-gun, thought Rott, Bennish and Mac were right, the terminals weren't damaged, he would be able to reroute them with the spare cabling he brought.

"Captain. I've identified the damaged cables and am about to replace them."

"How long do you think it will take?"

"About ten minutes," estimated Rott. "But you'll know the second I fix it as the power storage meter should spike for a second."

"All right," said Bennish. "We'll watch for that. Carry on."

Rott planted his feet firmly in a position that allowed him to work comfortably. He detached the severed ends of the cables from their terminals and began replacing them with cables and sheathing from his toolkit. It was exacting work, made more difficult by the wearing of gloves, and sweat started to pour down Rott's brow. He reached for the suit's temperature control and cranked the cooling system. The burst of cold air on the back of his neck was exhilarating and, with newfound strength and stamina, he connected the last replacement cable.

With tools back in the toolkit, Rott turned and began the walk back to the access door. He was about half way there, with the opened door in sight, when he felt the ship shudder three times in quick succession. In the vacuum of the housing, he could not hear any external sounds that could help him identify the source of the shudder, but, like a forensic investigator, his mind processed the available evidence: his location; the ship's operating procedure; and his relationship, or lack of it, with the ship's captain. There was only one logical conclusion. His blood suddenly ran as cold as ice.

Rott's worst fear was realized when his eyes confirmed what his mind had deduced. The access 'vault' door had closed, the exhaust vent door was opening, and Main Thruster Four was warming up for ignition.

18.
TRIAL BY FIRE

The monitor flashed and the icons and text that graphed the power storage meter reset to zero, cycled through some numbers, then settled on a specific reading.

"Did you see that?" exclaimed Bennish excitingly. "It reset, just like that bastard said it would."

"Well that's good news, right Captain?" suggested Mineko. She was hoping to instill some form of happiness, no matter how small, into Bennish. He was exuding a nefarious aura of doom and gloom. It was palpable. Mineko could sense something dreadful was about to happen. And she was right.

"Close the access door," commanded Bennish.

Mineko, bewildered, turned and looked up at Bennish. "Rottweiler's still in the housing, sir."

"I'm aware," said Bennish, his voice the epitome of controlled anger. "Now close the access door, open the exhaust vents and prepare for limited forward propulsion. And before you think about questioning my orders remember that all crewmembers, even you, are expendable."

Mineko noticed that Bennish was now gripping his pistol and his index finger was stroking the trigger guard. She swallowed hard. "May I at least ask why, sir?"

"Someone's been deleting strands and contaminating the re-instantiation materials."

"Oh my God. Who?"

"Who do you think?" said Bennish angrily. "Rottweiler. Why do you think I sent him out there?"

"Maybe we should talk to him."

"For what, to tap into his inner feelings? Jesus Christ! The guy's ruining our mission." Bennish shook his head. "You're too soft, Minami."

"That's not true."

"Then why do you carry a picture of your family and rub it like a goddamn security blanket?"

Mineko opened her mouth to reply then sat in stony silence.

"That's right," said Bennish coyly. "I saw it."

"It doesn't compromise the mission," pleaded Mineko.

"Mementos were to be left behind." Bennish's voice started rising. "That was an order you accepted. Doesn't disobeying orders compromise a mission?"

"But it's only a picture! It's trivial!"

"And if someone is compromising the entire mission by deleting strands and sabotaging materials is that trivial too?" screamed Bennish.

"No, of course not," said Mineko as she cowered in her seat.

"Then stop fuckin' with me and follow orders!" Bennish drew his pistol and started banging it on the console in time with his rant. "Close the access door. Open the vents. Engage the thruster. Now! Now!"

Mineko quickly entered the three commands, and a little bit more of her humanity, her soul, had been poisoned by Bennish.

* * *

When a person realizes they are about to die, worse, about to be murdered, their mind becomes a mumbo-jumbo of disjointed thoughts. The parts of the brain (thalamus, hippocampus, sensory cortex, etc.) concerned with self-preservation, the 'fight or flight' response, has to weigh and evaluate the circumstances, the pros and cons, of standing ground or forming a path of escape. And it does this in a millisecond. But during that time, the body's automatic response to fear, the emotion caused by outside stimulus that triggers an instinctive, autonomic response, kicks into gear.

The sympathetic nervous system sends out impulses that cause the adrenal medulla to release adrenaline and noradrenaline, the stress hormones, into the bloodstream. Heart rate increases, pupils dilate, muscles tense, nonessential systems shut down, and the brain focuses on the immediate threat, diverting its resources from trivial matters to the only thing that matters: survival.

And Rott's body was no different from the hundred billion homo sapiens that preceded him since the dawn of man. It reacted to this threat, the entrapment in a main thruster housing that was about to be flooded with white-hot plasma, the same way Neantherdal man reacted when he realized a wild animal had entered his cave. And like that man in the cave, Rott's 'fight or flight' response was hampered by one irrefutable fact: there wasn't any escape route available.

Rott screamed into his helmet. "Why are you doing this?"

"You thought you could delete strands and we wouldn't find out?" said Bennish incredulously. The words emanated clearly from the speakers in Rott's helmet, but his brain, soaked in fear and wrapped in unbridled terror, heard the words in waves of garbled sound, as if he was underwater. His mind had to process each syllable, each word, and assemble it in an order that made sense. And since his brain couldn't comprehend why this was being done to him, it could not accept the translation.

"What are you doing to me?" Rott looked desperately around the housing. Maybe he could try something. Maybe he could run to the thruster's exhaust hole. The vent door was open. No. The blast of plasma would turn him into an ember. Maybe he could hide somewhere in the housing. Somewhere where the incredible heat that would radiate from the thruster wouldn't reach him. Impossible, there was no such place. There was only one thing left to do. Eliminate the threat. Stop the perpetrator.

Rott's sensory cortex, realizing the only plan of action was to reason with the person instilling the fear in him, detoured resources to his power of reason and speech.

"Captain," pleaded Rott. "Why are you doing this? I've done nothing wrong."

"Deleting strands and putting Nutroxen in recombinant components is nothing?"

Rott heard a slight rumble coming from the thruster. Jesus Christ, it's going to fire!

"Captain! Captain! No! No! It wasn't me! I swear to God it wasn't me!"

"'Extinction is what we do'," said Bennish. "Your words, not mine, Rottweiler. And may you burn in hell forever. Bennish out."

It was inevitable now. And in this position of facing certain death, of knowing that in about one minute his body was going to be incinerated, Rott's brain broke down and gave the signal for his body to carry out one last task, one pathetic attempt at stabbing back at the evil Bennish and the bastards on the ship that had wronged him.

Rott made his way back to the power cables he had just repaired. Like a mindless automoton, he reached into his tool belt and retrieved the cable cutter. He then proceeded to sever every cable within reach. And as he cut the last cable, and as he felt the freight train-like vibration under his feet that signaled the ignition of the plasma, he threw his cutter at the thruster and yelled, "Fuck you, Ben-"

The thruster ignited and Eric 'Rott' Rottweiler was instantly incinerated. The young man from Nebraska, the teen that dreamed of better times beyond his farmland, the salmon handler and engine/power specialist, the one-of-six humans chosen to save humankind, was reduced to a black smudge on an engine housing seventy million miles away from his home planet.

* * *

"It was an assassination, nothing less."

Mineko was addressing Mac, Sandra, and Van Lank as they all sat around the table in the Ready Room, nervously waiting for Bennish to make his appearance at a meeting he called to order. Mineko, knowing she only had a minute before he joined them, provided the others with a quick synopsis of what had happened to Rott.

Mac removed his cap and rubbed his hand through his hair, then placed the cap back on and pulled the bill down practically over his eyes. "Jesus, Rott was a traitor. That son-of-a-bitch had me fooled. I never smelled a rat."

"Well, that's the key to putting a fox in a henhouse, isn't it? Pick someone that no one will suspect," Van Lank explained.

"Thank God you ran those tests, Sandra," said Mineko as she leaned forward to get a better view of Sandra, which was being obscured by Mac's bulk in the chair next to her. "You must've shit when you saw the Nutroxen show up."

"More like vomited," said Sandra flatly. "To think that someone I worked with, that I trusted, was working against me, against us, made me sick to my stomach."

The Ready Room's door slid open and Bennish marched in and took a position in front of the table. His stance was a bit unsteady; his gaze a little less focused than usual. When he spoke, one could sense that each of his words was being enunciated with some labor, like a tonsillectomy patient requesting his first morphine drip. There was no way for the crew to know that Bennish's repeated drug injections had caused a median palatine cyst to form in the center of his hard palate. This hindered his tongue's movements and distorted his words.

Though Sandra wasn't privy to Bennish's predilection for drug abuse, she had a strong sense he was a user, and that theory was shared by the other crewmembers. She wished she could somehow obtain a sample of his blood; she would have loved to run a tox report on it. But that opportunity hadn't presented itself yet. She hoped that it would.

"I'm sure Minami has told you her version of the events regarding the late, great Eric Rottweiler," said Bennish calmly. "Now I'll tell you the truth. Rott was a traitor, a cancer to this mission. He was deleting strands and he introduced Nutroxen into the re-instantiation cylinder. Who knows what he was going to do next. I had him in a position of tactical weakness and I eliminated the threat. Minami, here," Bennish waved a dismissive hand in her direction. "Minami wanted to bring Rott back in for a talk. You know, to discuss his childhood and somehow blame his parents for his shortcomings and then have some kind of group Commie hug. I do things a little differently. I shoot first then ask questions later."

"Sir," said Van Lank with all the deference he could muster. "I know all of the circumstantial evidence points toward Rott, and I'd be the first to agree that any traitor needs to be disposed of summarily, but do we have any hard evidence that Rott's the one that deleted the strands or sabotaged the components?"

"Any person or thing that compromises the integrity of our mission, for any reason, will be disposed of," said Bennish, his calm cool visage starting to crack, like an ice sculpture on the first day of spring.

Is this guy bipolar or what, thought Sandra, as she sat, amazed, at the self-centered Bennish waxing on poetic with his 'integrity of the mission' spiel. She wondered when the unstable ass-hole would tear off the respectable captain mask and reveal himself. When would Mr. Hyde appear? If she were a betting person, she'd expect the appearance any second now.

"I understand that," explained Van Lank. "But did you have irrefutable evidence or were you basing it on Rott's defense of The Chrysander's view?" Van Lank was treading on thin ice and he knew it.

"Jesus Christ! This isn't a friggin' court of law! On this ship you're guilty until proven innocent. The slightest suspicion is good enough for me!" Bennish placed his knuckles on the table and leaned into the four, flushed faces. "And I'm the one wearin' the badge. Don't any of you forget it!"

Bingo, thought Sandra.

Mac, knowing he was on Bennish's shit list as it were, decided to make a desperate attempt at gaining brownie points. "I'm sure we all agree with that, Captain. But Rott was our power expert and Mineko said we're still a bit short of the levels you want. Anything we can do to help out?"

At first, Bennish shot a glance at Mac that could melt a glacier, but he softened for some inexplicable reason. Inexplicable to everyone except Bennish, that is, for Bennish had walked into the meeting knowing he was going to have to order one of the crew to carry out a physically grueling chore, and Mac had just volunteered himself.

"I'm glad you feel that way, Mac, cause I know a way we can generate power. It'll take the strength of ten men. But since we're short a man and the rest of us have our own responsibilities to attend to, you're going to have to do it on your own."

* * *

You really put your foot into it this time, Mac thought to himself as he opened the service bay door located above Main Thruster Two's housing. Usually, he would've looked forward to a space walk, but not now, not like this.

When Bennish had explained to the crew how he wanted to make up for the lost power levels, no one could argue with him, for his logic was sober and the plan was sound.

Located deep in the bowels of the *Prometheus*, in one of the hundreds of massive warehouse rooms, lay a store of parabolic mirrors that were destined to be attached to the ship's exterior once it landed. The mirrors were designed to act like giant magnifying glasses, multiplying any available light by a magnitude of over one hundred thousand. The resulting light would be concentrated into laser beams, which would enter the hull through specially designed holes. The beams would then excite diamond fused photovaic cells, and these, in turn, would convert the light into enough electricity to power a small city.

The crew agreed that one mirror, even deployed in the darkness of space, would be able to convert enough ambient light into a beam strong enough to compensate for Main Thruster Four's impaired production. Granted, during entry into the New World's atmosphere, the mirror would be sheared off like a flower petal in a hurricane. But NASA's engineers had also included the parts necessary for the New

World inhabitants to construct a small geothermal power station, so the loss of one mirror was not a concern.

And now, here was Mac, saddled with the arduous task of schlepping one mirror and the associated hardware to its attachment point above Main Thruster Two's housing. It was slow work. For one thing, Mac had to rely on the magnetic boots, which made for slow going. And once he shouldered a part to its destination, he had to secure it to the hull before he could retrieve the next one. But by taking it one step at a time, the seconds turned to minutes, the minutes turned to an hour, and it was with both a sense of relief and accomplishment that Mac finally mounted the five foot diameter parabolic mirror onto its motorized, adjustable mount.

Mac retrieved a polishing cloth from his kit and began to clean the translucent lumiglass mirror. A faint reflection of his helmet's visor stared back at him, distorted as if from a funhouse mirror. Mac knew that once power was sent to the mirror, the glass' illuminessence particles would become positively charged, turning the glass into a jet-black mirror, and the light magnification would begin.

"Captain," said Mac, exhausted. "The mirror is installed and has been wiped down."

"Good job, Mac," said Bennish truthfully. "We'll open the panel to the lens bay. Clean the lens then bring it in. You've been out there long enough."

"Roger that," replied Mac.

Visible on the hull, about ten feet directly in front of the mirror, was the faint outline of the six-inch square panel. Mac squatted before it and waited. After a few seconds, it slid into the hull, exposing a space about as big and deep as the proverbial breadbox. Taking up the bulk of the interior was the smooth oval lens of the photovaic cell. Mac kneeled down and began to polish the lens. "Dammit!" he spat.

"What's wrong, Mac?" queried Bennish.

"It's the lens. An air bubble must've been caught in the lens when they poured the mold."

"You gotta love low bid work," said Bennish. "How bad is it? D'ya think it will affect the cell's function?"

Mac studied the lens carefully then turned clumsily in his suit and looked over his left shoulder at the mirror that was directly behind him. "The bubbles toward the port side of the lens, if the mirror calibrates itself properly, the beam should hit the center of the glass and avoid-"

"Hold on a second, Mac," interrupted Bennish. "I have an urgent message coming to me from Hapgood. Take a breather. I'll be right back."

Mac sat back on his haunches, exhausted. He thought about the iced tea he was going to have once he re-entered the ship. English breakfast tea, some dehydrated lemon and honey, and plenty of ice. He could almost taste it. It wasn't exactly the large, peach-flavored iced tea he used to get at his local donut shop's drive-thru every morning while in college, but it was a close second.

This reverie about one of life's simple pleasures was broken by the sound of Bennish's voice. "Mac, I'm back."

If Mac hadn't been so tired from his exertions, he might've noticed the change in tone in Bennish's voice. Instead, he said weakly, "Is Hapgood all right?"

"Oh, she's fine. Just reporting in. Let's finish checking the lens. Besides the bubble, let's check for other imperfections. Slide the cloth around it slowly and tell me if it snags."

"Roger." Mac leaned forward, reached into the lens bay and slowly, methodically moved the cloth over the lens. "Smooth so far. No sign of- ARGGGHHHH!" screamed Mac horrifically.

If Mac hadn't seen what happened to his wrist, if he had been looking away and had to venture a guess, he would've surmised that someone had dropped a guillotine's blade on it. But he did see what happened, clear as day. And the pain was so blinding, so mind-numbingly intense, that he expelled a bit of vomit onto the inside of his visor. For the lens bay panel, the small, sliding ceramisteel door that could withstand the force of a ship's liftoff and landing, had closed like a vice on Mac's right wrist, compressing it to one fourth its normal thickness.

And though Mac was still in shock, he was able to hear and comprehend the words that poured into his ears, courtesy of Captain Kalin Bennish.

"Mac, remember I told you that Hapgood had an urgent message? Well it was really bad news. Bad news for you, anyway."

19.
LET THERE BE LIGHT

When Sandra Hapgood had left the Ready Room meeting earlier, it was with mixed feelings. On one hand, she was relieved that the threat to the strands, and to the crewmembers themselves, appeared to be over. No strands had been deleted since Rott was neutralized (or assassinated, depending on who was telling the story, Bennish or Mineko), but, on the other hand, she still wasn't one hundred percent sure that Rott was the culprit.

Sandra made her way to the Strand Extraction Lab. She wanted to prepare the sampler gun for when the crew would need it the following day, if they stuck to their schedule. Sandra decided not to put the altered sampler gun, which was used against the humanoid, back in service. Even though she could disinfect it and re-engage the retaining clip, she'd feel better introducing a new one into service.

After retrieving a new sampler from a cabinet, Sandra began to tear off the vacuum-sealed wrapper. She stopped when she noticed that it was torn in one corner. Sandra immediately examined the edge of the cabinet door, hoping to find a bit of wrapper snagged on a rough edge. That way, she'd be relieved to know that she had just caused the tear, as opposed to being paranoid and believing that someone else had done it earlier, compromising the sampler's integrity. When her examination of the door proved negative, she stared at the sampler gun. Should I use it or not, she asked herself. There were still two other samplers in the cabinet. But what if they were compromised also but the perpetrator had found a way to seal the bag again? This was ridiculous; she now didn't even trust new equipment!

Sandra tossed the sampler aside and grabbed another new one. She tested it for a full hour then loaded it with a strip of Lexan tubes and attached the data cable. She slid it into its slot, put her hands on her hips, and slowly surveyed the room. She wanted to memorize the position of everything, so that on her next visit she would notice if something had been touched. Satisfied that she was now prepared to play this solitary game of 'Concentration' on her next visit, she left the room and made a beeline to the Strand Data Room.

Upon entering, she stopped dead in her tracks, for the display wall monitor was again delivering bad news.

STRANDS INSTANTIATED:	5,052
CORRUPTED:	1,083
VIABLE:	3,969

"Jesus Christ," muttered Sandra as she ran and half stumbled into her seat, "What the hell is going on here?"

Sandra engaged the intercom. "Captain Bennish?"

Mineko's voice answered. "He's speaking with Mac right now."

"Tell him it's urgent!" exclaimed Sandra.

A moment later, Bennish's voice could be heard. "What is it?"

"It wasn't Rott," said Sandra. "It wasn't Rott," she repeated on a diminishing scale.

Silence on the other end for a second, then Bennish spoke again in a clipped tone, "I'll take care of it. Right now."

Sandra slumped in her chair for a second but then hunched over the keyboard and swiped more commands.

Evelyn's picture appeared on the monitor. The green border, that signified its viability, brought an audible sigh of relief from Sandra. She stepped away from her chair, took one last look at the monitor, then made for the exit. She wanted to meet with Van Lank. She needed a video surveillance system deployed in the Strand Data Room, and she needed it deployed now.

* * *

A lightning bolt of pain shot through Mac's arm as he tried in vain to wiggle his hand free from the steel trap of the access door. But a lightning bolt lasts for a millisecond. This pain was relentless. A million nerve endings were fighting for the brain's attention, signaling their predicament, and waiting for him to give the return signal that would remove them from the stimulus. But there would be no such signal. Like the sacked quarterback whose face was being plowed into the grass as time ran out, there would be no last second comeback, no Hail Mary pass that would save MacNamara.

And as his brain went into a mild shock, the pain lessened enough for him to hear Bennish's words through his helmet's speakers.

"You've been a bad boy, Mac."

Mac could understand the words, but couldn't understand how they applied to him. When Mac spoke, his words came in halting syllables, as he was taking quick breaths in between each word. "What, what do you mean?"

"Bringing banned videogame systems on board…"

"You broke my hand for that?"

"Hacking into environmental controls, with my password, no less. Then graduating up to deleting strands…"

Mac was dumbfounded. "What do you mean? What are you talking about?"

"You thought you could get away with it, eh?"

"Get away with what? What evidence do you have?"

"Thought I'd let you ruin the mission, did you?"

"I didn't ruin anything, what gives you the right to accuse me?"

And then Mac heard Bennish, in an off key voice, begin singing, "Daisy, Daisy, give me your answer do…"

At that point, Mac knew he was targeted for elimination. Not by some treacherous computer in a sci-fi film, but by a deranged Captain in the now defunct Air Force of the United States of America.

"You sick bastard," cried Mac. "You're the murdering son-of-"

"Minami, activate the mirror," ordered Bennish.

"But, sir, Mac's right in line with the beam it will produce."

Mac didn't need to hear Mineko's assessment of the situation, he knew better than anyone that if the mirror was activated, it would immediately amplify any available light and send a white hot laser beam right through his chest. It would then bounce off the ceramisteel access door, as it was covering the beam's normal target, the lens. The reflected beam would then travel thousands of miles through space until it dissipated.

Mac was only concerned with getting his body out of the way, but his trapped hand and arm acted as an anchor, cementing him in harms way. If only he had a cutting tool! He could cut his arm off and escape the death beam. Hell, animals chewed their legs off when caught in traps, and other humans had dismembered themselves to escape from sure-death situations.

Wait a moment! He did have a cutting tool. He could do it! With his left arm, Mac reached into his tool kit and extracted a cable cutter. Its jaws wouldn't open wide enough to cut his arm off in one fell swoop but, if he didn't pass out, he'd be able to do it in about four snips.

"Minami. Activate the mirror immediately or face the consequences."

"I won't. I won't do your dirty work anymore."

That's it, thought Mac, keep fighting him, Mineko. Delay him long enough and I'll get myself out of this. I don't care if I'm maimed and bleeding like a stuck pig, I'll strangle that bastard with my one good arm. I'll save the ship. I'll save the mission.

Mac had maneuvered the cable cutter so he was holding it firmly in his left hand. He opened its jaws wide and grabbed a good hunk of the inner part of his elbow. He figured that it would be easiest to cut through the soft flesh and tendons first, then use the cutter to crack the elbow joint apart. Mac heard a 'thump' emanate from his helmet's speakers and some sort of gasp or moan from Mineko. Don't think about that, he said to himself, just squeeze your left hand and make the first cut. You're running out of time!

In 1905 in France, Dr. Beaurieux observed the decapitation of a convict named Languille, and the good doctor reported that "Languille's eyes very definitely fixed themselves on mine and the pupils focused themselves." The doctor thus concluded that a quick fatal blow, like the devastating strike of a guillotine blade, does not kill a person instantly; there is still about ten seconds of awareness of one's horrific death. Unfortunately for Daniel MacNamara, he was about to join this macabre club. For just as Mac was looking down at his elbow, a thin, continuous beam of glowing yellow light exited his sternum area, bounced off the ceramisteel access door, and shot off into space.

How extraordinary, thought Mac. I see the beam going through my chest yet I'm still conscious. How can this be? Of course, the heat of the beam has created a cauterized tunnel right through my body. Ha ha! Bennish thinks he's killed me, but he hasn't. The fool picked the wrong weapon. Wait'll he hears my voice. He'll shit! Now, what should I say? What words will shock that son-of-a-bitch the most? I know. I'll tell him I'm coming for him. Plain and simple.

And as Mac opened his mouth to speak, everything went black. He slumped forward then sideways. The white-hot beam made a clean cut from Mac's sternum, through his scapula, and up to his clavicle. It then cut straight across the back of his neck. Mac's head, still encased in a NASA helmet, separated cleanly from his body and floated off gently into space. From the moment the beam entered Mac's body until the moment he lost consciousness, thirteen seconds had elapsed. Dr. Beaurieux would've been impressed.

20.
THE CHAIN OF COMMAND

Bennish watched as Mineko slumped in her seat. The lump on her forehead, delivered by the butt of his pistol, started to swell aggressively. He reached across Mineko's body and flipped the switch that would activate the mirror. The back of his hand was resting against Mineko's left breast. He could feel it gently moving up and down in step with her shallow breathing.

Bennish turned his hand over and kneaded it. No response. Man, he had thumped her good! His whole shoulder was behind the blow when he delivered it. His father would've been proud.

Bennish contemplated the zipper of Mineko's jumpsuit. He grabbed its tab and slowly, lovingly, pulled it down to her navel. He looked at the two beautiful snow-white mounds that were being restrained by the black bra and swallowed hard. He subconsciously shifted his stance to relieve the constriction his underwear was exerting on his groin. When that didn't help, he decided to relieve the pressure another way.

He'd take Mineko to the Strand Extraction Lab and force her onto the gurney. Then once he ravaged her viciously, he'd put the gurney in motion and have it evacuate her body. He'd tell Van Lank and Hapgood that he had discovered Minami was Mac's accomplice and he had to eliminate the both of them. His twisted mind, which had lost all sense of reality due to a combination of mental illness and two days of intense drug use, actually believed this to be a good plan.

"Minami," said Bennish as he slapped her face. "Wake up."

Mineko groaned and opened her eyes. For a second she had trouble focusing. But when Bennish pointed his pistol directly into her right eye, she became alert. "Whatever you want, you don't need the gun. We can talk about it," she said calmly.

"I want you in the Strand Extraction Lab," said Bennish. "And the gun ensures I get you there. As for talking about it," Bennish started chuckling. "Well, in a few minutes, you won't be able to talk about anything."

* * *

"My God. I think Bennish just killed Mac!" Sandra looked at Van Lank to gauge his reaction.

"I think you're right," replied Van Lank. "I think our friend Bennish has gone off the deep end."

When Sandra had left the Strand Data Room a few minutes earlier, she made her way directly to the Planet

Assessment Room, where she found Van Lank fine tuning his planet searching algorithms.

"Have you been listening to this?" asked Van Lank as he pointed to the speaker on the wall.

Sandra cocked her head to listen. She heard Mac speaking.

"I didn't ruin anything, what gives you the right to accuse me?"

And the minute she heard Bennish sing 'Daisy, Daisy, give me your answer do...' she cursed, for she had known Mac's taunting of Bennish with his *2001: A Space Odyssey* insult, would come back to haunt him. But how far would Bennish go?

Sandra and Van Lank sat there like two statues, ears straining for every sound, every syllable of the horror that was unfolding on the hull outside of the ship. And once they heard the 'thump' and Mineko's moan, they both surmised that she had been incapacitated by Bennish, so that he could activate the mirror at will.

"We have to go help Mineko," said Sandra.

"We will. But first we need a plan. Have you isolated the Strand Data Room's computer from the others?"

Sandra shook her head and looked away from his gaze. "No. Every time I try to take it out of the loop, I lose permission to access any strand data at all. I have to find some way for my workstation to think it's still communicating with the others, then there'll only be one access point to the data." Sandra raised her head and looked at Van Lank. "Have you come up with a video surveillance system yet?"

"No," replied Van Lank. "But something Bennish said a minute ago intrigued me. I have to look into it first, but if things go the way I think they will, I should have a system soon."

"Well, that will take care of one problem, but what are we going to do about Bennish? He's a mentally unstable whack job…and I'd bet my life he's a user on top of it. What if he's The Chrysander's mole?"

Van Lank bit his lip. "Bennish doesn't give a shit about anybody but himself, so I don't see him doing The Chrysander's bidding and trying to destroy humankind. Bennish is an egotistical megalomaniac. He'd want as many people possible to make it the New World, for no other reason than to have a bunch of minions to rule over."

"But what if he was brainwashed? What if he's doing the bidding and not even realizing it? The Chrysander knew more about altering thought processes than anyone else. He had some of the world's top behaviorists, psychologists and microbiologists swear allegiance to his cult. If they got a hold of Bennish and overrode certain synaptic structures, he'd never even be aware of what he was doing."

Van Lank jumped out of his seat. "In a way, that's good. That means we can still reason with the conscious side of him. Or at least we can try. Come on. Let's go."

Sandra and Van Lank made their way to the cockpit and, seeing it empty, made a beeline to Bennish's quarters. The door was unlocked so, after knocking numerous times, they entered. The empty room sneered at them. As they turned to leave they noticed that something under the bed was reflecting the light from the corridor.

Sandra bent down and picked up a small, empty, bottle. She rolled it in her hand then sniffed the top. "Hallucinogenic. He's been injecting himself. For all we know he's high as a kite right now." She dropped the bottle, made her way out of the room, and started jogging down the hallway with Van Lank on her heels, checking every room they passed. "We have a lot to thank the Air Force and NASA for, picking this ass to run the most important mission in human history," said Sandra sarcastically.

"What were those idiots thinking?" muttered Van Lank as they arrived at the door of the Strand Extraction Lab and stepped through. From the other side of the divider, they heard the sound of someone pulling their pants up and fastening a belt. Van Lank put his finger to his lips and motioned for Sandra for follow him quietly. They tiptoed to the edge of the divider and slowly poked their heads around. They were not prepared for the sight that greeted them.

Mineko was sitting on the gurney. Her jumpsuit was unzippered down to the navel and had been pulled back around her, so that her arms were effectually trapped behind her back. Her melon-sized breasts were bared and big red welts shown around her areolas. An angry red welt shown on her forehead and some green spittle was drooling from her lips and joining a puddle of pea-green vomit that was pooled at her feet. She looked up at the two voyeurs as a caged shelter dog will look up at a potential new owner. She tried to talk but could only mouth the words: Help me.

Standing beside her, buckling his belt with his right hand, was Bennish. His left hand was holding his pants up and also awkwardly holding onto his pistol. As casually as one would swat a fly, he backhanded Mineko with his right hand. She rocked backwards then came forward again. A fresh burst of vomit splattered on the floor.

"Quiet!" ordered Bennish.

"Stop that!" said Van Lank firmly.

Bennish looked at the two interlopers and continued as if neither had spoken. "Don't mind her. She can't talk right now. Her throat's all fucked up." Bennish laughed heartily. "And now that the show's over, we have some work to do. Hapgood, prepare the sampler gun."

Bennish had become serious all of a sudden. He gestured with the pistol, first pointing at Sandra and then at the sampler. Sandra turned to Van Lank for guidance and as he nodded his agreement, Bennish roared. "What are you looking at him for? I gave the order!"

"Captain, what do you want us to do?" asked Van Lank calmly.

Bennish was now moving the gun back and forth between Van Lank and Mineko. "I don't know who else here is in cahoots with Rott and MacNamara; who else is intent on ruining my mission. Every time I think I have the perp, more strands get deleted. I'm not taking any more chances. I'm going to have Hapgood strand the two of you and then test your cores to see if you've been brainwashed. If she finds nothing, I'll let her re-implant them."

"But Captain," pleaded Van Lank. "That's a destructive procedure. It wipes away the tapped cortex. You'll be lobotomizing us. We won't be able to help you fulfill the mission."

"There may not be a mission unless I do this. Hapgood, start with Minami here. She won't put up much of a fight."

Sandra pulled the sampler gun from its slot and positioned herself in front of Minami.

"Sandra!" yelled Van Lank. "You're not thinking of actually doing this, are you?"

"Ryan, honey, I promised a beautiful young girl that I would see this mission through. This is bigger than you and Mineko, this is for the continuation of humankind." Sandra placed the muzzle of the sampler against Mineko's forehead.

"Sandra, don't let him do this, he's killing us one by one. You know that." Mineko's voice was weak but audible.

"Listen to her, hon. Think about what you're doing," implored Van Lank.

Though Sandra had the muzzle of the sampler resting against Mineko's forehead, she hadn't pulled the trigger yet.

Bennish was becoming agitated. "Come on, Hapgood. Let's go!"

"Sandra, please don't do this," pleaded Mineko.

"Do it!" ordered Bennish.

Sandra looked into Mineko's eyes. "Relax. You won't feel a thing."

And in one fell swoop, with lightning quick speed and precision of movement, Sandra swung the sampler towards Bennish's forehead and pulled the trigger. He dropped to the ground like a load of bricks. His pistol skittered across the floor.

Van Lank quickly rushed to Sandra's side and kissed her on the cheek. "Well played. Very well played."

Bennish was laying face up, his arms and legs at odd, unnatural angles, for he had crumpled to the floor like an abandoned marionette. His eyes were open and he was making gurgling sounds. A Lexan tube half jutted out of his forehead.

Sandra Hapgood put the sampler down and helped Mineko into a standing position. She pulled her jumpsuit back around and zipped it up. She handed Mineko a towel and pulled a cold bottle of electrolyte water from a refrigerated cabinet. Mineko took it greedily, untwisted the cap, and put the bottle to her lips. She drained the contents in a single draught. She crumpled the plastic bottle and dropped it on Bennish's stomach.

"He's still alive, isn't he?"

"Yes," said Sandra factually. "He can't move but he can still feel, hear and think."

Mineko smiled a smile that would've made Genghis Khan's blood run cold. She reached for the sampler gun and squatted down on the ground. She spread Bennish's legs as far apart as possible and pushed the muzzle of the sampler deep into his groin.

"What you're feeling right now is the barrel of the sampler gun. I have it resting up against what my high school physiology book called 'the male reproductive system'. I'm going to engage the trigger in a few seconds and a plastic tube is going to slice through your scrotum, testis, prostate, and then come to rest in your bladder. You will bleed out and you will bleed out badly. You will feel pain that you never knew existed; but it won't kill you. What will kill you is the next shot. I intend to open your mouth and place the barrel of the sampler as deep down your throat as possible before I shoot its load, sorta like what you did to me a few minutes ago. You know, an eye for an eye and all that."

Behind Mineko, Van Lank unconsciously crossed his legs. And then Mineko carried out her revenge, her pay-back. And as she withdrew the sampler's barrel from the mouth of Bennish's corpse, Sandra queried her. "Orders, Captain?"

Mineko tossed the sampler aside, picked up the pistol, then turned to exit the room. "Evacuate his body and core samples. I don't want one bit of that son-of-a-bitch left on this ship."

21.
A CRUSHING DEFEAT

Breakfast was Sandra Hapgood's favorite meal of the day. Since her days in college, she would rise at 6:00am, head to the cafeteria and order the same meal, day in and day out. She would then grab a seat by the window and consume the one egg (over easy), a high-fiber English muffin (topped with grape jam), two strips of bacon (preferably honey-maple), and a flavored iced coffee (usually vanilla crème or chocolate glazed donut). Sandra continued this ritual during her time at NASA and, after noticing Mineko ate her modest meal of yogurt and banana at the same time, invited Mineko to join her each morning.

So it was, on the morning after Bennish's forced removal from power, Sandra and Mineko joined each other once more for breakfast. Sandra had to forego her beloved fried egg, but she placed a bowl of reconstituted egg product into the microwave; it would make a reasonable facsimile of scrambled eggs. And as her muffin toasted she mulled over the box of individual, coffee flavored K-Cups, finally choosing the 'coconut/almond/chocolate' one. She placed it in the brewer and, while it expelled the thin, steaming stream of the candy-bar smelling coffee into the ice filled cup, she reached into the refrigerated cabinet and grabbed a bottle of orange juice and a container of yogurt for Mineko.

When her meal was ready she placed everything on the table as, like clockwork, Mineko entered the room. They sat and ate and talked about the events of the previous day. And though they both spoke freely and emotionally, each of them was hiding a secret from the other.

For Mineko, it was the change in her personality, in her belief in herself, and the mission, that she was shielding from Sandra. For the events of the previous evening had had a profound effect on Mineko. When she had left the Strand Extraction Lab, she headed towards her quarters. The sobbing started as she was halfway there and by the time she opened her door, she was blinded by a river of hot, salty tears. She stripped out of her clothes and stood in the shower, mouth wide open, trying to gargle away the taste of Bennish. As she rubbed the soap on her bruised and battered breasts, she cried out, for the pain brought back a flood of memories. Mineko took the bar of soap and pounded it against the shower wall until it turned into a frothy mushroom, at which point she flung it towards the drain.

Once she exited the shower, she put on a robe and sat on her bed. She fished into her jumpsuit pocket and extracted her Disney World photo, which she stared at intently. What had happened to that eight-year old girl, the one dressed as a princess and smiling so innocently into the camera? What would that little girl think of the person she was now, someone that had contributed to the death of fellow crewmembers because she had been too weak to disobey orders? Someone that had killed a man, for the love of God, castrated a man?

Mineko always prided herself on being a good, decent human being, and yet she was now no better than the executioners in the French Revolution or the guards at Dachau. Maybe all humans had this evil, this propensity for death and destruction hardwired into them. And here they were trying to seed another planet with the same flawed human species that had ruined one planet. Were they crazy?

Mineko now hated that picture in her hand. Hated how it promised happiness, love and joy. Hated how it caught a moment in time that would never, ever happen again. She tore the picture into tiny pieces, flushed it down the toilet, flung herself on her bed, and cried herself to sleep.

And now, here she sat in the Galley, conversing freely and hoping Sandra wouldn't notice that her heart and soul had been ripped from her body.

But Sandra also had a secret, and it too concerned Mineko, for Sandra intended to murder her within the hour.

* * *

After Sandra and Van Lank watched Mineko execute Bennish and exit the Strand Extraction Lab, they placed his body on the gurney and engaged the ejection system. They watched in silence as the gurney disappeared into the wall. As soon as the next gurney positioned itself, Van Lank turned to Sandra and, with a sly smile on his face, slapped his hands together and said, "Well, that's that!"

"What a treacherous asshole," sneered Sandra.

"We have to make sure now our mission is a success. We owe it to the memory of Rott and Mac, and to Mineko for the hell he put her through."

"You're right, Ryan. Listen, I'm going to take his core sample to the lab and test it for alterations. He was either an unwitting accomplice to The Chrysander or he knew exactly what he was doing. Either way, it doesn't matter, but I'd like to know."

"And I'd like to look over the contents of his quarters, maybe I'll find something incriminating. And I also want to follow up on something Bennish said about Mac," Van Lank looked at his watch. "What if I meet you in my quarters in about, say, two hours?"

"I'll probably be later than that. It'll take about an hour and a half to check Bennish's core, then I want to go look at the strands before I go to bed."

"Okay," replied Van Lank. He gave Sandra a quick kiss. As he left her he turned and said, "Smile. The nightmare's over."

I truly hope so, thought Sandra as she donned some surgical gloves, removed the Lexan tube that contained a mix of Bennish's brain, groin, and throat samples, and left the room.

She walked the deserted corridor and entered the Medical Clinic, where she spent the next two hours performing chemical and microscopic analysis of Bennish's brain tissue. She checked and double-checked her data. Satisfied with her results, she made her way to the Strand Data Room. And once more, her heart stuck in her throat when she glanced at the monitor.

STRANDS INSTANTIATED:	5,052
CORRUPTED:	2,304
VIABLE:	2,748

"What the frig?" screamed Sandra as she rushed to her seat and entered some commands on the keyboard. Evelyn's picture zoomed to the forefront of the monitor. Its green outline brought the usual sigh of relief from Sandra. She stared at the screen for a second then turned to the history computer. She engaged the record button and spoke into it.

"Evelyn. We've had some problems on this journey. Some people on board don't understand the importance of our mission and they're doing some stupid things that put the strands in danger. But you're not to worry. I've prioritized your data so it's the most protected one. And you'll be the first person I bring back. I promise. And you, me, my future husband and, if things go as planned, my future child, will all live happily ever after together. Now, I've got to go and take care of a few things. Bye for now."

Sandra spent a moment ensuring that the revolving security codes, that were preventing all of the strands from being deleted at once, were still operational. She then left the Data Room and headed directly to Van Lank's quarters. She found him dozing so she shook him forcibly.

"Ryan! Ryan wake up! It's not over."

Van Lank opened his eyes wide and sat straight up. He shook his head and rubbed his face. "What is it?"

Sandra quickly explained that Bennish's core showed no sign of manipulation and that the strands were still being deleted.

"I would've sworn it was Ben-" Van Lank stopped in mid-sentence then hit his forehead with the palm of his hand. "Son-of-a-bitch. Of course, how could I have been so blind?"

"Ryan, what are you talking about?"

Van Lank grabbed Sandra by her shoulders. "I checked out Bennish's room tonight. Found dozens of bottles of drugs-"

"Yes, I know," said Sandra. "I checked his core sample. He was practically living on hallucinogenics."

"But I also found something else. I was looking on his pad, I got by the password screen with his serial number, and I found a journal app. It was like a diary. And as I skimmed through it, I found a few entries where he reminisced about meeting with The Chrysander and his minions, and discussing how to sabotage the mission-"

"So there you go," said Sandra. "You found the smoking gun."

Van Lank shook his head. "No, no. You don't understand. The incriminating sentences seemed like they were shoe-horned into his normal entries. And they didn't read like Bennish spoke. They were too, um, feminine. It's hard to explain, but I think a female wrote those entries and planted them into his journal."

"But why? Who?"

Van Lank started rocking gently. "We've been so blind, so blind." Van Lank stopped short and stared at Sandra. "Think about this: Who's the person that told us that Bennish was assassinating people?"

"Mineko," answered Sandra.

"Right. And who's the person that was sitting right next to Bennish? The one that carried out his orders and killed the space station crew and killed Rottweiler?"

"Mineko…" started Sandra. "But wait a minute. We heard her on the intercom arguing with Bennish when he wanted her to activate the mirror that killed Mac."

"Of course, she had to fight back at some point. But she could afford to. She knew that Bennish would end up activating it himself if she disobeyed his order. She just didn't figure on receiving such a severe reprimand. And then she tells you to get rid of Bennish's body and core samples. She didn't even want you to check them for synaptic manipulation."

Sandra rubbed her face then clenched her fists over her eyes. "But that could've been because she was so mad at him, she probably wasn't thinking clearly." Sandra pulled her hands off her eyes. "I can't believe it. I can't believe Mineko would do something like this."

"This has nothing to do with what Mineko would do or not do. If she's been brainwashed she's clueless as to what she's been doing."

A full minute of silence passed between them before Sandra posed a question to Van Lank, in a subdued voice that suggested she already knew the answer. "So what do we do?"

"I hate to say this, but we have to eliminate Mineko. If we don't, she'll eventually eliminate us…and the remaining strands."

"Well, we can't just walk up and overpower her. She has Bennish's gun now, remember?"

Van Lank rested his chin between his thumb and forefinger. "I think I have a plan that will throw her off guard," said Van Lank as he put his hands behind his head and leaned back against his pillow. "Just long enough for you to kill her."

And now, as Sandra finished her breakfast, the plan that Van Lank had formulated was repeating itself over and over in Sandra's head. She drained the last of her iced coffee and turned towards Mineko.

"Would you be able to help me check the cylinders in the Recombinant Labs? I want to make sure before we go into stasis tomorrow that everything's up to spec."

"Of course," replied Mineko.

Both women stood up simultaneously, gathered up the remains of their breakfasts, and placed them in the refuse bin. They headed down the hall and entered Recombinant Lab Two. Like Lab One, it was basically a large circular room with a giant steel cylinder in its center.

"Ryan tried to fix the door of Lab One's cylinder but couldn't. That humanoid practically tore it off," said Sandra. "So it's important that the other nine labs are in perfect order. I want us to be sure that Nutroxen wasn't introduced into any of the other cylinders."

Sandra grabbed a handful of sterile swabs from the nearest countertop and handed them to Mineko. "While you swab the protein feed pipes inside the cylinder, I'll check the external connections."

"Okay," agreed Mineko as she grabbed the swabs and stepped into the cylinder.

Sandra pretended to check the exterior of the cylinder as she spoke to Mineko through the opened access door. "I disobeyed one of your orders."

"Oh," said Mineko jocularly as she swabbed the interior of one of the nutrient feed pipes. "I don't remember giving any, so you'll have to remind me what it was!"

"The one where you asked me to evacuate Bennish's body and core samples. I decided to check them for alteration or signs of brainwashing."

"Oh, well, yes, I mean I guess that was a good idea on your part. I wasn't thinking clearly," said Mineko, a bit flustered.

"Interesting thing," said Sandra as she inched her way closer to the access door. "I didn't find any sign of manipulation."

"Well, he must've just been an asshole," joked Mineko.

"But Ryan did find phony entries in Bennish's journal."

"Wha-, what do you mean?"

"Entries meant to implicate him as The Chrysander's conspirator."

"That's unbelievable. That means Mac or Rott must've done it," said Mineko nervously.

By this time Sandra had maneuvered herself so she had her right hand on the door handle and was looking at Mineko through the opening between the door and its frame.

"Ryan says the entries were written by a female. And that female was you."

Mineko, who had been looking up into one of the protein feed pipes, now turned and looked, wide eyed, at Sandra.

"And you know what," said Sandra, her eyes fierce with anger. "I believe him."

Sandra Hapgood immediately slammed the door shut and engaged the outer locking mechanism. She turned and ran towards a control panel that rested on one of the cabinets that encircled the outer perimeter of the room. She could hear Mineko pounding on the door of the cylinder and screaming, "Sandra! What are you doing? Let me out!"

Ryan's plan was about to be concluded. Sandra slammed her fist down on the big, red 'Test' button. This would send high pressure streams of proteins, minerals, and water into the cylinder. Electrical and chemical stimulants would then bombard the mixture to create a non-living gelatinous mass. It was the only way to test a cylinder's pumps and fuses. Ryan had determined that, due to the acidic nature of the hydrochloric stomach acid that would normally be re-instantiated last in a strand brought back to life, a person like Mineko caught in the still swirling mix would be incapacitated within seconds.

Sandra turned and looked at the cylinder. Through the glass window she could see the whirlpool of water and colored proteins. She could not see any part of Mineko nor hear any screams.

Sandra immediately heard what she thought was a bolt of thunder and felt something fly by her head, clipping her ear. She turned to see the cylinder's door lock sticking out from the wall panel behind her like a coat hook. She turned back towards the cylinder and saw Mineko step out. Her shiny, straight black hair clung to her face, which was red and raw. Her eyes were bloodshot and weeping terribly. Her jumpsuit, which had been dark blue, was now faded, almost white, and it was giving off either smoke or steam. And as she walked towards Hapgood, she raised the gun and pointed it between Sandra's eyes.

"I still have two shots left," said Mineko as she strode slowly, like a panther sizing up its prey.

Sandra looked towards the exit of the room and, seeing she'd never make it in time, did all that she could do; she pulled a large chair away from its nook in the cabinet and ducked down behind it.

"Sandra, I can't believe you fell for Ryan's lies, implicating me. It's probably him that's doing this. I bet that's why he's even with you, to stay close, to know when you're sleeping, to learn how to delete the strands." Mineko stopped about fifteen feet away from the chair and lowered the gun. "Now come out and we'll talk about this, we'll confront Ryan, and then I'll kill him!"

Sandra desperately grabbed the chair by its arms. She figured that when Mineko got close enough, she could lift it and throw it at her. It was a weak plan with hardly any chance of success but it was the only one she had. She tensed her muscles and attempted to lift the chair a bit, so that she'd be able to toss it at the right moment. It was like lifting a bag of cement! It wouldn't budge.

Both Mineko and Hapgood heard a sound at the entrance. They turned and saw Van Lank's shoulder and arm duck back out of the room. All of a sudden, Mineko's feet lifted from the floor and she started to float towards the ceiling. Sandra started floating also. Ryan must've reached in, unlocked the environmental controls, and lowered the gravity. The chair would now be weightless!

As Mineko fired off a precious shot at the retreating arm of Van Lank, Sandra lifted the chair as if it were a balloon, and flung it with all her might. It caught Mineko full in the chest and sent her tumbling towards the ceiling, which she hit with such force she released her grip on the gun. It floated away and was joined by floating balls of multicolored protein soup, which were now escaping from the cylinder's open door.

Mineko squatted on the ceiling then propelled herself toward Sandra, who had been tossed against the wall by the reactive force of the chair toss. Their bodies met with incredible force and bounced off the wall, about twenty feet above floor level.

Van Lank, holding tightly to the doorframe, stepped into the room and planted himself firmly so he could manipulate the gravitational control. He raised it back to 'normal'. Immediately, everything in the room dropped like rocks. Both Mineko and Sandra groaned and tried to get up off the floor, two punch-drunk fighters both waiting for the other to be counted out.

Van Lank noticed that the gun had landed closest to Mineko and she was reaching for it, but he also noticed that Sandra's right hand was resting right next to an electrical access panel on the floor. "Sandra! Hold on to the panel's handle!" he yelled as he lowered the gravity setting to minimum.

Mineko immediately flew up and was flattened against the ceiling, her head making a loud cracking sound. Sandra was flung straight up into a cartwheel position; feet pointed towards the ceiling, right hand desperately holding onto the handle.

Van Lank set the gravity to normal and Mineko came crashing down to the floor. The sound of bones crunching could be heard. But she would not be stopped that easily. She rose to her feet, her back to the cylinder's open door, and screamed an animalistic scream. Sandra had also made it to her feet and she was now standing face to face with the enraged Mineko.

Van Lank lowered the gravity setting just as Sandra hauled her right arm back and, with all her might, hit Mineko square in the nose. It exploded into a stream of red, floating balls of blood and Mineko shot backwards into the still active cylinder as if she had been fired from a cannon.

Sandra immediately pushed off with her feet and dove for the cylinder's door, which she shut and leaned against with all her might. "Put the gravity to normal!" she screamed.

Van Lank made the adjustment, which allowed Sandra to plant her feet firmly on the ground and hold the door shut. The swirling proteins and elements could still be seen clearly in the window. They could both hear grunting noises coming from within the cylinder but they became less frequent after a few seconds and finally stopped. Once the cylinder completed its test cycle, Sandra opened the door.

Mineko Minami, or what was left of her, was slumped on the floor. Of her skin and jumpsuit there was no sign; she resembled those skinless, preserved bodies that used to draw crowds in science museums, but this body was also covered in a gelatinous film. Sandra thought she noticed a flutter in the heart and lung area. She leaned her head in a bit further but then pulled back when she realized it was only Mineko's body, settling.

Sandra turned away from the cylinder and picked up the gun. She ejected the last live round and tossed it and the gun into the cylinder. They landed with a soft 'thump' on Mineko's remains. Sandra walked towards Van Lank, grabbed his hand, and led him from the room. She leaned back in, set the gravity setting to maximum, then quickly leaned back out. Almost immediately, all the items in the room imploded, flattening themselves with a horrible crunching sound. The steel cylinder vibrated for a second then accordioned onto itself, a thousand gallon soda can stepped on by an unseen giant.

And Mineko's remains, splattered like a bug, shot out from the base of the crushed cylinder, and littered the floor.

22.
THE VISITOR

"We haven't learned anything, have we?"

Sandra rolled over and looked into Van Lank's eyes, searching for an answer.

"Do you mean us or humans in general?" said Van Lank, propping himself up on one arm.

"Can you separate the two? Look what we've done. We've killed each other off. We extinct each other. It's what we do."

"The strands will begin again. Maybe this time they'll get it right," said Van Lank hopefully. "Maybe one of them will be a leader that represents peace and hope and joy. I would've once thought it would be you or me, but we're tainted now."

"The strands are nothing but everyday humans, a bunch of men, women and children with their own faults and needs, their own dirty little secrets and their hatreds and prejudices. I met them all, granted for only a few seconds,

215

but none of them struck me as being the next Ghandi or anything."

Van Lank smirked.

"Strike that," said Sandra. "One person did have something special. Something that struck me as a genuine good hearted soul, embodying the best of a flawed species."

"You mean Evelyn, right?"

"Yes," said Sandra. "And I've promised her that she'll live in the apartment next to us, and our child hopefully. All four of us living in some foreign, alien world." Sandra laughed derisively. "Boy, that'll make for a normal childhood, some place with two suns and five moons or something." Sandra closed her eyes tightly and put her clenched fists to her forehead. "My God. What have we done?"

Van Lank stroked Sandra's hair. "Remember that picture I painted? The one whose location you've been trying to guess for the past two days?"

Sandra looked up. She rubbed a tear from her eye. "Yes? What about it?"

"Well, I wasn't being fair to you. There wasn't any way for you to guess so I'm going to tell you. It's a place called Shangri-La, the most beautiful place in the universe."

"Shangri-La is a fictional place," retorted Sandra. "A place we all aspire to visit, another Xanadu or Garden of Eden."

"It's real, Sandra, and you're going to see it," said Van Lank excitedly. "You see, all those hours I spend in the Planet Assessment Room, all those hours I spend tweaking the criteria for the planet this ship decides to land on, all those hours are spent so I can achieve one goal: for humankind to start fresh on that place I painted."

Sandra looked at Van Lank with real excitement. She sat up quickly in the bed. "Tell me about it!"

"Well," started Van Lank and he put his arms behind his head and leaned back. "This ship is going to land within a mile of the most beautiful, white sand beach man has ever seen. The sky will be so blue, so intense that every day, we'll all look up and marvel at its beauty. There'll be fresh water nearby and an abundant supply of edible fruits and vegetables. There'll be fish in the sea and small game in the forests. The soil will be hardy and the rainfall will be just right; no flooding but no droughts either. The temperature will average seventy-two degrees. And we'll be able to use the wood from trees to build boats, so that we can travel to other parts of the New World. Areas with snow and mountains and lakes and fields."

"It sounds absolutely beautiful," said Sandra as she cuddled up to Van Lank. "I almost wish the next eighty years were over and we were there already."

"Remember, it's going to take a lot of work, a lot of team work among the surviving strands. We're going to be short handed now that some of the strands are no longer viable. By the way, how many strands are left?"

"Two thousand, eight hundred...wait, I mean, two thousand, seven hundred...Oh My God! I can't believe it, my mind is mush. I've lived and died by these numbers and now I can't even remember!" Sandra jumped out of bed.

"Wait! Where are you going?" asked Van Lank.

"To the Strand Data Room. I'm going to check the number."

"Sandra, get back in bed. Don't go in there again until I'm with you."

"What? Why? What are you talking about?"

Van Lank patted the bed next to him. "You'll see tomorrow morning; a little surprise. Come on, it's been a stressful day. Let's get some sleep."

Sandra shrugged her shoulders and climbed into bed. She didn't want to. She really wanted to run to the Data Room and count every single strand, but she realized that Ryan had spent the last few minutes trying to console her and put her mind at ease. She didn't want him to think that he had failed. She climbed into bed and cuddled next to Van Lank. Within ten minutes, they were both asleep.

She awoke abruptly a few hours later. She had dreamed that Mineko was whispering in her ear, suggesting again that Ryan was the traitor, was the real culprit behind the strand degradation. It seemed so real that when Sandra woke and sat up in bed, she looked at the sleeping Van Lank with aversion and distrust. She realized the folly of experiencing these emotions due to a dream, but they had dug a pit in her stomach.

Sandra gently, quietly (stealthily?) slid out of the bed and tiptoed out of the room. She stopped by the Galley, put a Crème Caramel K-cup into the brewer, and quickly made herself a steaming cup of coffee. She entered the Strand Data Room, noticed that the sea of red photos hadn't grown, settled into her seat, placed her cup in the chair's holder, then stared at the monitor. She wanted to memorize the number of viable strands. She read them aloud. "Two thousand, seven hundred and forty-"

Out of the corner of her eye, Sandra noticed a reflection of movement on the history computer's screen. She hadn't heard any accompanying sound so she dismissed it. "Two thousand, seven hundred and forty-"

There it is again, and this time I know I saw something, thought Sandra. She looked over both shoulders in a vain attempt to see behind her, but the high back and sides of the chair impeded her view. She twisted her chair around, half expecting to see that Van Lank had snuck into the room, probably to talk her back to the comfort of bed.

But there in the center of the room, holding a long whip in his hand and preparing to strike, stood The Chrysander.

Sandra's shoulder took the brunt of the landing as she dove out of her chair, a split second before the tip of the whip struck the chair's headrest. She rolled to a stop and quickly got to her feet, assuming a defensive position, arms raised and prepared to defend her eyes and face from the cracking whip.

"How'd you get here?" asked Sandra in a voice reeking with hate and disgust as she looked into The Chrysander's eyes, his blank stare utterly devoid of emotion.

In lieu of answering, The Chrysander smiled wryly and raised the whip once more.

"How'd you get on board?" screamed Sandra.

The whip came flying towards Sandra's midsection. She dove over it, somersaulting onto her back then rolling into a standing position.

"So you've been deleting the strands. Who's been helping you?" A thought roared into Sandra's head and she immediately felt a brick form in her throat and stomach.

Didn't Ryan state just a few hours ago that he had a surprise he wanted to show her in the Data Room. Was this it? Was Mineko right? Was Ryan the traitor?

Sandra was so devastated by these thoughts that she wanted to give up, to sit down and let The Chrysander's whip wrap around her neck. She would then watch The Chrysander's arms strain as he pulled it tightly, causing her tongue to lag out of her head, her eyes to bulge from their sockets, and her lungs to strain for the breath that would never come. Then the final jerk of the whip and her neck would snap like a strand of raw spaghetti.

Frig that, thought Sandra. Everything you've worked for, everything you've done in life that brought you to this mission, is now in jeopardy because of this asshole. This guy wants to see humankind die right here on this ship. Well it ain't gonna happen. Not in this room. Not on this ship. Not on my watch!

And with a burst of energy borne from the inner reserves that are present in all natural fighters, Sandra rushed at The Chrysander and, with a primal scream, jumped into the air. Her right leg shot out at the intruder's face, a perfect sidekick that would've made Bruce Lee proud.

Sandra's aim had been dead on, so she couldn't understand why her foot, leg, and torso shot straight through The Chrysander's head as if he was made of air. Startled and off balance, Sandra crashed to the floor in an ungainly heap and rolled across the floor, hitting the wall with a thud.

Dazed and now vulnerable to The Chrysander's attack, Sandra looked towards the door as she heard footsteps approaching. When she saw Van Lank run into the room, her first thought was, 'How am I going to fight two of them?'. But Van Lank ignored The Chrysander and came right to her side. "Are you all right?" he asked wild-eyed. Before receiving his answer, he ran to the far side of the room, picked up a shoebox-sized item, and flipped a switch on it. Instantly, The Chrysander disappeared into a puff of holographic smoke.

Van Lank placed the box back down, then ran back to Sandra and propped her into a sitting position.

"It's Mac's virtual reality generator," explained Van Lank, the words running out of his mouth quickly. "It's part of the security system I was going to design. I rigged it so The Chrysander would attack anyone that tried to access the strands in this room."

Sandra pulled away from Van Lank. She looked at him warily. "Why'd you choose him?"

"For poetic justice," said Van Lank sheepishly.

"Way too little too late, Ryan," said Sandra, looking at him suspiciously.

"It wasn't until I heard Bennish reprimand Mac for having a video game system that I knew the perfect thing to cannibalize."

Sandra still eyed Van Lank guardedly. "Why the whip?"

"A whiplash is the strongest type of sensory feedback it can generate." Van Lank's face suddenly lit up. "But look what it can do now!" He walked back over to the V.R. Generator and pressed a button. "Watch this!"

Sandra turned in time to see a virtual Van Lank appear in the center of the room. When it spoke, it sent goosebumps up and down Sandra's body, for it was if another Van Lank existed, real as life.

"Hi, Sandra. You're watching a recording I made of myself a few hours ago. What do you think?"

Sandra shook her head slowly and turned to the real Van Lank. "What good is this thing now?"

Van Lank reached down and turned the generator off. He walked over to Sandra and, realizing she wasn't in the mood for him to touch her, stood there awkwardly, looking for some place to put his hands.

"It might not be good now, but it will be great when we have a child in the New World. Think of the home movies we'll be able to make."

Van Lank's enthusiasm was just slightly contagious. Sandra softened, approached Van Lank and rested her hands on his shoulders. "I'll admit it's better than 3D," said Sandra with a smile. "But do you really believe we'll think of the New World as home?"

"A city becomes the world when you love one of its inhabitants. Remember?" said Van Lank as he kissed Sandra lightly on the lips.

"I do." Sandra returned the kiss, took Van Lank by the hand, and led him towards the exit.

As they approached the doorway, Van Lank stopped and grabbed Sandra's upper arms from behind, holding her so she could not turn and face the room's interior. "So tell me," said Van Lank jocularly. "How many strands are viable?"

"Um, two thousand, seven hundred and forty---something!" said Sandra light-heartedly.

"Close enough for government work," said a winking Van Lank.

They shared a rare laugh and left the room.

23.
FRIEND OR FOE

Sandra slept soundly and peacefully. She dreamed of the New World, the New World as Van Lank had described it. It was thriving with humans, humans that were laughing and smiling, even as they toiled in open fields under the warm sun. It truly was Shangri-La.

Sandra rolled over, her arm flopping across Van Lank's pillow. It took a second for her subconscious to wonder where Ryan was. She woke with a start. Van Lank was not in bed, nor was he in the room. Maybe he had gone back to his own quarters. No. Most likely he's tweaking his planet assessment criteria. He really was obsessed with ensuring that *Prometheus* would zero in on the most perfect planet in the universe. What an example of single mindedness and dedication. Speaking of dedication, guess I should go check on the strands.

Walking toward the Strand Data Room down a deserted corridor was disconcerting. My God, how quiet it is without Mac, Bennish, Mineko, and Rott. It's like a ghost town. That's okay. Ryan and I will be in stasis soon and the next time we wake up, we'll be re-instantiating hundreds of others. Soon I'll be complaining it's too crowded in here! Sandra smiled to herself and turned into the Strand Data Room.

No one would have faulted Sandra for what she did next, for the sea of red photos was a dead giveaway that almost a thousand more strands had been corrupted since her last visit, leaving only a little more than a thousand of them viable. Her legs turned to jelly and she faltered in her step. Her mouth opened and closed like a fish out of water. "How, how, can this be?"

The wall monitor displayed the following information:

STRANDS INSTANTIATED:	5,052
CORRUPTED:	3,846
VIABLE:	1,206

Wide-eyed and trembling, Sandra looked around the room frantically. There it is, she thought, the V.R. Generator. Ryan said it would record what had transpired in the room! Sandra ran towards it, got down on her knees, and was about to hit the 'rewind' button when she saw the power switch was turned off. "Dammit!" she spat. She bit her lip and desperately looked around the room. "Think, dammit, think!"

Sandra ran to her seat and immediately swiped some commands. Evelyn's picture zoomed to the front, it's green border confirming its viability. Sandra stared at it with fervent concentration for a good two minutes then, having made up her mind, she sprung into action. She shut down the history computer and popped off its plastic housing. She carefully extracted its hard drive and placed it on her desk. She then swiped some entries into the Strand Computer and looked up at the wall monitor. She read the words aloud. 'Strand Data Room, Hard Disk 17, 100% Corruption.'

Sandra ran to the other side of the room, human history hard drive in hand, and popped off a wall panel, which revealed a bank of twenty hard drives, all numbered sequentially. She ran her finger up and down the disks until she came to number 17, which she then extracted and tossed on the floor. She took the history computer's hard drive and inserted it.

Halfway there, thought Sandra. She ran back, sat down, and entered some commands into the Strand Data Computer and looked up at the monitor.

COPY DATA OF EVELYN HIMMEL TO DISK 17? YES OR NO?

Sandra entered 'yes' and watched the thin blue bar appear on the screen, it elongated from left to right as it mapped the progression of the copy command. She held her hands tightly together under her chin, willing it to copy faster. "Come on! Come on! Damn you!"

About one tenth of the way across, the blue bar abruptly stopped and an alert appeared on the screen. It stated the following:

HARD DRIVE IS FULL.
DISK SPACE NEEDED: 19 ZETABYTES
DISK SPACE AVAILABLE: 2 ZETABYTES

"Shit!" screamed Sandra. She stared off into space for a few seconds then turned back to the keyboard and typed furiously. The wall monitor then flashed, in big red letters, the following words:

ERASE HUMAN HISTORY DATABASE?
YES OR NO?

And Sandra swallowed hard as she chose the affirmative action. And again, a blue bar appeared, elongating from left to right as it displayed the progress of the deletion of the database that contained the history of humankind. My God, thought Sandra, what am I doing? Thousands of years of drawings, works of art, literature, science, all being deleted in about ten seconds, and all because of some half-baked scheme I have that isn't even guaranteed to work. She begged God's forgiveness.

With the database deleted, Sandra was able to successfully copy Evelyn's strand onto the hard drive. She removed the drive from its slot, put it back in the Human History Computer, and replaced the computer's plastic housing. She then turned it on and swiped some commands.

Satisfied that a pristine, viable copy of Evelyn's strand now resided on, what once was, the Human History Computer, Sandra leaned back in her chair. Yes, human-kind's history was gone but the human species still had its chance at survival, a fair tradeoff.

But now Sandra had to face the fact that strands had been deleted as she slept, and Ryan Van Lank was the only suspect. It was one thing to be betrayed by someone you love, thought Sandra, but when that someone is the only other human being alive, it was especially painful. And how would she know if he was an active agent of The Chrysander or an innocent brainwash victim? If she stranded him and tested his core sample, she'd lobotomize him. No. She'd go to his quarters (Sandra was sure he'd be in the Planet Assessment Room) and rummage around; see if she could find any evidence.

And with her mind made up, Sandra Hapgood made her way to the V.R. Generator, turned it on, and exited the room.

She made a beeline to Van Lank's quarters. It was empty, so she quickly yet methodically searched where she could: in the closet, in his pad's journal entries, in the chest of drawers, etc. Nothing! Wait a moment. He wouldn't hide anything in the open. If he did have incriminating evidence he'd lock it away. Yes, of course, his footlocker! The lock box that he's had since he was a teenager. He had once asked Sandra to retrieve something from it about a month ago. He had given her the passcode! Please God, tell me he hasn't changed it!

Sandra pulled the lockbox out from under the bed and concentrated. What was that code? Think. Think. Wait. It was his birthday backwards and forwards! With a finger trembling so badly she almost missed the buttons, Sandra typed in 6-2-1-1-2-6. The box top sprang open and she delved through the contents. There! What's that sheet of pink paper folded and shoved in that envelope?

Heart pounding, Sandra pulled the paper out and quickly unfolded it. It was one of The Chrysander's promotional flyers! Her hand started shaking as she gazed at the small picture of The Chrysander, hand raised high in a gesture of victory. The guy thinks he's Hitler, thought Sandra. Repulsed by the visage of this madman, Sandra threw the pamphlet to the ground as if it were on fire.

So, it wasn't brainwashing. Ryan was reading this crap, hiding it, probably pulling it out and swearing allegiance to The Chrysander. Wait a minute. Didn't Ryan recreate this madman in holographic form using the V.R. Generator? Didn't he tell me it was for 'poetic justice', meant to appear and frighten whoever was deleting the strands? What bullshit! Ryan probably thought it would be poetic justice for The Chrysander's image to be present when he deleted the last strand, when he murdered her, the last crewmember! That bastard!

And now that she knew that her lover, correction, her former lover was guilty of the attempted extinction of humankind, a crime that no court would acquit and no God would forgive, she knew that she would have to eliminate Ryan Van Lank. But how?

Sandra scanned the room's items; the watercolors, the old books, the old-fashioned ink blotter, letter opener and stapler. Wait! That's it, the letter opener. It was about as long as a steak knife. She tested the edge. It wasn't razor sharp but it would make a suitable stabbing weapon. Sandra slid the opener up her sleeve and left the room.

The sounds of her footsteps echoed off the empty corridor as she ran, first to the Planet Assessment Room, which was unoccupied, then to the Galley. Van Lank was sitting at the table, sipping an orange juice and reading a novel, *Path to Eternity*. The remains of a scrambled egg breakfast were set before him.

Van Lank saw Sandra enter the room. He looked up and smiled. "Hey. I thought I'd let you sleep in."

"How long have you been here?" asked Sandra accusingly.

"I don't know. Why? What's the matter with you?"

"What's a matter with me? With me? You murderer!" screamed Sandra.

"Sandra, I don't know what you're talking about," said Van Lank calmly.

"A city becomes a world...what shit!" said Sandra as she pulled the letter opener from her sleeve and held it menacingly.

"Sandra, come on, what are you doing? Let's talk about this." Van Lank picked up his napkin and dabbed his lips. He purposely placed it down next to his fork, which he deftly palmed. He then slowly pushed his chair back from the table and stood up.

"No more talk. I can't let you delete any more strands." And with that, Sandra thrust the opener towards Van Lank's throat. But he was prepared for the attack. He quickly brought his fork forward and caught the opener's blade in its tines. He pushed the opener away and slashed back at Sandra's throat with the fork.

"So, it's come to this," said Sandra as she ducked and backed away.

"We haven't come very far, have we?"

"Rott said this is what we do: extinct each other." Sandra started circling Van Lank, shifting the opener from one hand to the other.

"I don't want to hurt you," said Van Lank as he joined the deadly dance by maneuvering his feet to keep Sandra at arms length.

"You've already torn my heart out, there's no other way you can hurt me." Sandra lunged forward then pulled back, striking like a snake.

"Sandra, please, put that thing down. I don't want to kill you."

"Don't worry," said Sandra confidently. "You won't."

And with that, Sandra thrust the opener towards Van Lank again. He took one step back then used his right leg to throw a crescent kick at Sandra's head. But Sandra had anticipated the kick and dove to the floor. In one quick movement she sliced the Achilles tendon of Van Lank's left foot. He dropped to the ground as his ankle gave way and laid flat on the floor.

Van Lank was now defenseless, a turtle on its back. Sandra pounced on him and, using the opener as a dagger, prepared to plunge it into Van Lank's heart. But Van Lank used both of his hands to hold the opener just inches from its target. And right when the tip of the opener touched his jumpsuit, Van Lank flipped the opener around so it was now practically touching Sandra's neck. He slowly pushed it closer and closer to her pulsing Carotid artery.

"You'd kill the woman that would bear your child?" asked Sandra.

For a split second, Van Lank stopped pushing and looked into Sandra's eyes with a mixture of hope, for what might have been, and fear, for what was going to happen. And Sandra seized the opportunity. She flipped the opener back around and, with all her strength, slid the letter opener into Van Lank's chest.

Van Lank stared sadly at Sandra until his eyes glazed. He choked up some blood, then became still. Sandra could practically feel the life, the soul, leave the body. It was as if someone removed the air out of a balloon, or the spring from a wind up toy. One second this heap of water, proteins and minerals was a living, breathing human being, and now? And now Sandra had taken another life, the second one in twenty-four hours. The third if you counted Bennish. When Sandra met her maker, how would she account for the three notches on her belt? Well, she thought, I can't worry about that now. I have to think of the strands, of Evelyn.

Sandra began the task of moving Van Lank's body to the Strand Extraction Lab, where she placed it on the gurney along with Van Lank's books and watercolors. She pulled the painting of Shangri-La from the pile and took one last look at it. I wonder if this ship is even heading there, she thought. For all I know he may have planned for *Prometheus* to fly straight into a sun. Sandra engaged the gurney and as it slowly made its way into the wall she threw the painting onto it. She then walked out of the room and looked out the window.

Van Lank's body was slowly moving away from the ship. Sandra watched his books hovering around him. Like flies on shit, she thought. The Shangri-La watercolor floated towards her. It stuck to the window glass for a second then drifted away like a feather on a gentle wind.

And now to the Planet Assessment Room, to make sure the ship was really seeking out a planet that could support human life. Sandra tested the assessment computer by instructing it to scan and evaluate the nearest planet. The results were as follows:

HYDROGEN BASED ATMOSPHERE
LIQUID AMMONIA RAINFALL
DOES NOT MEET CRITERIA
WILL NOT SUPPORT CARBON-BASED LIFE

Well, thought Sandra, at least the computer is pro-grammed correctly. That's one mistake for The Chrysander. He should've brainwashed Ryan to crash the ship. This gives the strands, Evelyn, and myself, a fighting chance.

24.
AND THEN THERE WERE NONE

You don't know loneliness, true loneliness, until you are the last human alive in the universe. There is no one you can sit and chat with, or phone, or text, or email, or tweet. You can't even exchange a silent glance with the attractive stranger across the room.

No, the loneliness endured by Sandra Hapgood was the most intense that any human being had ever faced. Yes, some criminals, prisoners of war, earthquake victims, etc., were sometimes alone, but there was always hope. Hope that another human being would find them, talk to them, save them.

Sandra Hapgood was humanity's last hope. A sole human being traveling through the universe hoping a steel tube named *Prometheus* would plant her where life could flourish.

The greatest scientific minds had designed and built the Planet Assessment Computer, and the best scientific technician, Ryan Van Lank, had programmed it. But he had always joked that putting the *Prometheus* down on the correct planet out of the billions and billions that were out there, was the equivalent of flying in an airplane blindfolded, and dropping a white marble out of the aircraft's window, and having it land (two miles underwater, mind you) in a teacup on the Titanic.

If Sandra Hapgood worried about these things as she completed her chores aboard the ship, she didn't show it. For after evacuating Van Lank's body from the ship, she went room to room checking settings, examining status readouts, etc., all in preparation for when she would strand herself later that day. She knew she would die instantly and the gurney's gears would slowly rotate and ultimately eject her from the ship, but that was all right, that was the plan that she had helped formulate and bring to fruition. And after she checked the last room, closed the steel window shades, and double-checked the autopilot, she decided to have one last meal. Then she'd make the final visit to the Strand Data Room and the 'dead man walk' to the Strand Extraction Lab.

Sandra ate like a king. The microwaved meal was more than adequate. The lobster bisque was exquisite. The filet mignon was medium rare and melted on the tongue. The topping on her coconut cream pie tasted as if had been whipped just minutes ago. Her iced coffee (chocolate glazed donut flavor, her favorite) was delicious right down to the last ice-cube.

A heavy meal on top of a stressful day can make one tired, lethargic. Sandra yawned deeply and decided to take a powernap, so she'd be fresh when she completed her final tasks. Twenty minutes in bed and then she'd bring this mission home. She cleaned up her trash, made her way to her quarters, lain down on her bed, and was instantly asleep.

* * *

Sandra opened her eyes with a start. One glance at the clock informed her that she had slept one hour and a half, not just twenty minutes. Wow, thought Sandra, I must've been tired! She rolled out of bed and stood up. She didn't feel well. Her stomach was queasy and her head hurt. Sandra cursed the food processing plant that NASA had contracted for their meals; they should have pasteurized and irradiated the food better. She probably had a touch of food poisoning. Oh well, the good thing about being stranded is that she'd have a new body in eighty years or so, and the salmonella, if that's what it was, wouldn't be recreated in the re-instantiated body!

As she walked to the Strand Data Room, she wondered how many times in the last three days, in the last few weeks, in the last month she had entered this room. She was just about to try to figure it out when she walked into the room and froze. She stood as still as if she had been embalmed. Her mind couldn't process the sight before her. Every single photo on the wall monitor was bathed in red! There was not one viable strand! The monitor displayed the horror in pure simple text:

STRANDS INSTANTIATED:	5,052
CORRUPTED:	5,052
VIABLE:	0

Sandra rocked back and forth on her heels like a candle-pin waiting to drop after being skinned by the bowling ball. She finally broke out of her trance and ran towards the V.R. Generator. She knew she had left it turned on, trusted that it would record whoever had done this.

Like a baseball player rounding the bases, Sandra dove and slid to a stop, her hand touching the top of the Generator as if it were home plate. She pressed the 'rewind' button and held it for a second, then depressed the 'play' button.

The V.R. Generator came to life and projected a ho-lographic image of someone sitting in Sandra's chair. The chair's high back hindered Sandra's view; she could only see the left hand of the projected person as it swiped commands on the keyboard. Sandra took a tentative step forward.

"Bennish? Mineko? Ryan?" said Sandra incredulously. "But you're dead. You're all dead."

The V.R. Generator was recreating past events as realis-tically as possible. It projected the status of the wall moni-tor as it looked earlier when the video was recorded, when approximately one thousand strands were still viable.

And as Sandra continued her tentative steps towards the seated figure, she watched the once green rimmed, vi-able strand photos turn red, ten at a time. Sandra was livid. So this is how they were deleted, she thought. Someone had the gall to sit in my chair and delete my strands!

Sandra walked slowly, methodically, until she was al-most abreast of the chair. She still could only see the one arm and hand of the holographic image. Who was it? The suspense was mind numbing. Her feet felt like they were encased in leaden boots! Just one more step, she thought. She took a deep breath and quickly leaned forward, allowing herself to be face to face with the projection. And the person she saw, the person that had been corrupting and deleting strands since the mission started, was Sandra herself.

25.
CHECKMATE

Sandra stumbled to the floor, screaming, "No! It can't be!" Sobbing uncontrollably, she staggered to her feet and ran towards the V.R. Generator. She brought her foot back and kicked it with such force that, what didn't break from the impact, did break when it shattered against the wall. Sandra ran over to the pile of pieces and stomped on them, ground them into the floor.

Bile rose in Sandra's throat, gagging her. She was sickened that The Chrysander had chosen her, brainwashed her, so she would unwittingly assist him in his scheme to end humankind, the chess game to end all chess games. And she had been the pawn that just kept moving forward, taking out other, bigger pieces, more powerful than herself, until she cornered the opposing king. And The Chrysander had maneuvered her into this position so he could say 'checkmate' to humankind. Game over.

Sandra, carrying the weight of her guilt of complicity, collapsed under the strain. She fell to the floor and curled up in a fetal position. She cried over and over, "Why me? Why me? Why me?", until she thankfully, blessedly fainted.

* * *

When Sandra came to after fainting in the Strand Data Room, her mind was drowning in a whirlpool of memories. They came at her in waves, choking and gagging her with contradictions and lies, treacherous acts against her crew-members, her friends, for God's sake, even her lover!

It didn't take a rocket scientist (good one, thought Sandra) to realize that the night she went to The Chrysander's rally at the senior center, her beer was drugged. That meant Suzie, her friend that brought her there, was corrupt or brainwashed. Whatever. The beer knocked her out and she was taken some place where for the next few hours, The Chrysander's minions were able to subject her to the psychological and biological brainwashing process. But where? Someplace where they could work on an unconscious subject in private. Wait a moment. Where did we park the car? Of course, the Cozy Slumber Motel! How appropriate!

Sandra thought everything through. Okay, once on the ship it was easy for me to do The Chrysander's bidding. In the time it took Mac to run down the stairs to the air-lock, I had been there for ten minutes already, emptying the P.O.T.U.s of propellant. And the proliferation of fungus that Rott faced in the power room? Well, nobody knew more about fungus than I did, it was the first thing I ever stranded. I must've seeded those colonies with ease. And then Mac provided me with Bennish's environmental control password and I was able to crank the humidity in the

Power Management Room, causing the rampant growth that incriminated Rott. The entries in Bennish's journal, the ones that made Van Lank smell a rat, as he suspected a female's hand? That was me. The brochure in Van Lank's room? Me also. The deletion of the strands? Me.

And the worse thing of all is; my subconscious tried to warn me. That damn dream I had. Me coring apples while my twin, my mirror-image, sat there chewing, annihilating, strands of spaghetti, asking me if I really knew what I was doing. My God, why didn't I pick up on the clues?

And now? Suicide. It's the only rational thing to do. I have to pay penance. I've destroyed God's greatest creation, humankind, created in His image. I've murdered people in cold blood! I've destroyed humanity's last hope! What else is there to do besides suicide?

The Behavorial Health Lab. Sandra remembered the weekly Mental Stability Test that Van Lank would have had to take to prove his sanity if he was re-instantiated years too early. She knew that if he had failed, the room's door would lock, all oxygen would be extracted, and a potentially dangerous, crazed crewmember would be 'neutralized'. Why couldn't she take the test? Purposely fail it? Suffer a painful, choking death as penance, even though it would take twelve billion penances to pay off her debt to humankind.

Dammit, thought Sandra. It won't work! The test can't be administered until the ship finds an inhabitable planet, and that's still eighty-odd years away. Must find another way, another way to punish myself!

Sandra remembered a story that Mineko had once told her. If she recalled it correctly, Mineko's grandfather had been present when a Japanese general in World War II had

committed seppuku, or what Westerners commonly referred to as hara-kiri. The ritual had been attended by a
total of five people. And when the general unbuttoned his
tunic, and took up his short sword, he immediately cut his
abdomen left to right and then up towards the sternum,
and released his intestines. He had ordered his kaishakunin,
or assistant, to not deliver the standard decapitation, or da-
ki-kubi, but to let him sit and stare at his own intestines,
while he contemplated his failure to protect the Empire.

What a screwed up way of accepting failure, Sandra
had thought at the time, but now she understood the general's plight and identified with him. That might be the
way to go. Use Van Lank's letter opener! Poetic justice! But
then Sandra remembered that the general had died in a few
hours, and she didn't believe that would be long enough to
appease God, surely he would want her to suffer as long as
possible!

Upon further reflection she decided what to do. She
would force herself to eat, exercise, and take care of herself.
She would keep herself alive as long as possible in this steel
tube. Her penance would be the silence she would face each
day. The constant memories of her treachery would always
be at the forefront of her mind, as every room she entered
would remind her of insidious actions she had taken against
her fellow crewmembers.

She would not allow herself the luxury of visiting the
other five thousand plus rooms on the ship. Other than a
weekly trip to the deep freeze for food, her world would be
this floor only. She would be the bear in the circus that, after being caged in the ten-foot square cage for fifteen years,
was finally released into the forest and immediately started

walking in ten-foot circles, oblivious to the world around him.

But what to do about Evelyn Himmel's strand, the one she had so carefully saved by deleting humankind's history? Well, when Sandra reached old age, or when a crippling disease proved terminal, she would delete it. There was no way she would subject Evelyn to a life of solitude on some strange planet. Besides, the real Evelyn, the flesh and blood one, was killed two days ago by the strand sampler: the tool that Sandra at one point believed would save humanity. What arrogance!

And so Sandra started a ritual that she would follow day in and day out. She would wake at 6:00am and retire at 9:00pm. She kept her body in shape and the area cleaned. She'd eat three square meals a day. Every bite stuck in her throat but she forced it down. Must eat to stay alive, and stay alive to serve the penance.

And on one fateful day, two months after 'The Massacre' (as she had come to call it), Sandra ate her breakfast of scrambled eggs and bacon and immediately vomited all over the table. This simple human reflex of regurgitating food when one doesn't feel well, changed the course of humankind forever.

26.
REDEMPTION

The blood test result was confirmed with a second blood test, but Sandra still couldn't believe the diagnosis: pregnant; expecting; with child. The nausea was caused by a common human malady, suffered by billions since the dawn of man. Sandra had experienced morning sickness. She was carrying Van Lank's baby.

Half of her was ecstatic that a portion of Van Lank lived, the other half cursed God for making her responsible for yet another life. Now there was no way she could ever commit suicide, even if she wanted to, as she would be taking a life besides her own. And she had no intention of poking that stick in God's eye again.

And when Sandra reached the third month, she took the ultrasound wand and peered into her stomach. And Sandra Hapgood shed a tear when she saw she carried a baby boy. And in that billionth of a second, it was as if someone turned a light on in Sandra's head. She now realized something about The Chrysander and the role she played in his plan. Everything was clear now.

For the next five months, Sandra ate with gusto, took her vitamins, exercised gently. She'd sing lullabies aloud at night and recite long gone fairy tales during the day. Whatever portions she forgot she fabricated, always providing happier endings than the original stories.

And on the morning of February 24, 2027, at 9:00am, Sandra Hapgood entered the Strand Data Room. She sat down, took one last look at the sea of red photos, then entered a command. She reformatted all of the hard drives, essentially bringing the Strand Data Computer back to a new, pristine state, void of any strand data, of course. She then took the History Computer's hard drive and used it to transfer Evelyn Himmel's data to it. She then put the hard drive back into the History Computer.

She sat back for a second and double-checked her work. The Strand Data Computer was now functional and it contained Evelyn Himmel's strand. The History Computer was also functional, though it contained no human history. But Sandra picked up the microphone and recorded a lone entry.

"Evelyn. Evelyn. I saved you. Somewhere, somehow, for some reason. You see, I was chosen by a man known as The Chrysander that believed in humanity, believed that a fresh start would be the best way for humans, that were bent on destroying themselves, to begin again. I believe I was chosen, not to kill humankind, but perhaps to save it. Unfortunately, I can't make this journey with you, the events I've experienced have changed me. It's like I've run a marathon and now it's time for me to cross the finish line and collapse into the hands of others, into God's hands.

You're going to make it, Evelyn. I can feel it. But you'll have to start over. The history of humanity is gone. All that went before is gone. But maybe that's a good thing. Humankind will begin again, and this time you'll have a chance to form it, to make it better than before. So remember the best of humanity: our capacity for love, joy, and peace.

Now, I know that a few days ago I said you were on your own, but you're not. Every single human being that lived before you, your friends, your family, this crew, me, we'll all be pulling for you, rooting for you, praying for you, every step of the way. I won't say goodbye, as I hope to see you again in another time, in another life. So I'll say 'good luck'."

Sandra left the Strand Data Room and made her way to the Medical Clinic. She grabbed the portable ultrasound unit and wheeled it down the corridor and into the Strand Extraction Lab, where she placed it next to the Strand Sampler. Sandra stepped out of her jumpsuit and undergarments then grabbed a couple of extra pillows from the cabinet. She placed them on one end of the gurney, climbed up and leaned against them, as one will sit in bed when reading a book. She took the ultrasound wand and maneuvered it around her swollen stomach, staring intently at the display; she needed to know exactly where the baby's head was located.

Satisfied, Sandra shifted the wand to her left hand and, with her right, picked up the Lexan tube that was resting on the sampler cart and placed it between her teeth, as far back toward her wisdom teeth as possible, like a bit in a horse's mouth. Then, with her right hand again, she reached for the letter opener that she had sharpened that morning. She tested its edge against her finger. It was razor sharp.

After taking a deep breath and exhaling slowly, Sandra pressed the letter opener's blade against her stomach and carefully, painfully made an incision that quickly filled with blood. She looked at the ultrasound's display and began to cut deeper. It was only through sheer will that she did not pass out.

The blade showed as a black, triangular shadow on the display. When it came within an inch of the baby boy's skull, she quickly withdrew it.

At this point, Sandra began panting in quick little breaths, and the clenching of her jaw on the tube increased exponentially. Pieces of a molar shot across the room; shattered like a walnut in a nutcracker. Her jawbone was about to crack, she could feel it, but there was no turning back. She dropped the knife to the floor, reached for the strand sampler gun, and buried its barrel deep inside her belly.

Sandra, half conscious from the loss of blood, struggled to keep her focus on the display, but once she saw the muzzle of the sampler was resting against the center of her baby's skull, she knew she had done it, had succeeded.

Sandra engaged the sampler's trigger. She opened her mouth so wide to scream that the tube fell out, along with more pieces of tooth. She pulled the sampler gun, which was dripping with blood, from her mutilated stomach and placed it in its slot. Sandra fell back onto the pillows and sobbed in halting, weakening breaths.

On the monitor, a series of G, T, A and Cs, raced across and down the screen. After about a minute, the longest minute in Sandra's soon-to-be-over life, the letters stopped and the monitor displayed:

> DNA SEQUENCED
> SYNAPTIC MEMORY MAPPED
> SUBJECT'S NAME?

Sandra forced herself to turn towards the microphone that jutted up from the strand sampler. With her final breath she mumbled a name. If not for the microphone's speech recognition filter, the death rattle that then emanated from the back of Sandra's throat would've rendered the name a garbled mess. But the computer correctly identified the name Sandra intended and associated it with the strand it just encoded. And since Sandra had set the sampler into automatic mode, the same mode that she would've used had she been sampling herself, it automatically processed that data and engaged the gurney.

Within a few seconds, Sandra's body was ejected from the ship. The stream of blood from her stomach froze into a morbid, red icicle and, in a bit of irony, her outflung hand touched the same window, in the same place, that Evelyn's hand had bumped three days before. Then, one of the *Prometheus'* fins struck her body, like a cue stick hitting a billiard ball, and her corpse was flung haphazardly into deep space, never to be seen again.

* * *

The large black letters that had once spelled out *Prometheus* were now pitted and faded, as if they had been sand-blasted off the ship's ceramisteel skin. But the long-gone designers of the ship knew this would happen, expected it. For they knew that a flight lasting almost a century would subject the ship to abrasive meteor showers and interstellar dust storms. There had been nothing they could do to prevent the exterior of the ship from wear and tear, but they did have a plan for the interior. And that plan kicked into gear once the Planet Assessment Computer, which had been 'sniffing' passing planets for eighty-seven years, finally locked onto one that met the criteria that had been programmed into it.

Conditions inside the ship would've rendered its interior unrecognizable to its designers, for its appearance had altered dramatically during its long journey. Multiple strains of fungus, unimpeded by man, had flourished in his absence. Great, thick sheets of shimmering black and green gelatinous scum covered all ceilings, walls, and floors.

In the Galley, the K-Cup that had been left in the coffee brewer was the focal point for the growth. The brewer had sprouted five-foot plumes of brown and orange fungus, which touched the ceiling like some mutant, living stalactites. The Strand Data Room and Strand Extraction Lab were over run, individual pieces of equipment could not be identified, just different sized lumps under the undulating sheets of fungus.

In the Recombinant Labs, the tall steel cylinders glistened under the fungus colonies, while their interiors, due to the excellent sealing capacity of the cylinder doors, remained as clean as they were eighty-seven years before. Recombinant Lab Two was the exception, of course, for the organic remains of the long dead crewmember in the crushed cylinder had fed the fungus, encouraging incredible proliferation.

The display for the Planet Assessment Computer, which had been in long-term sleep mode, suddenly came to life. If there had been an observer in the room, he would've noticed the soft glow of the display, but the stream of text that was now appearing on the screen would've been illegible under the sheet of fungus. But the designers of the ship had planned for this rampant fungal growth.

The moment the display came to life, it was as if a bedside's morning alarm went off, for the ship 'woke up'. The thousands of sprinkler heads that dotted every ceiling in every room, released their store of Nutroxen. Like snow under a spray of hot water, the fungus literally melted away, their colonies instantly destroyed. After about ten minutes, grates in all the floors opened and the disinfectant/fungus mix drained away. Thermostats throughout the ship temporarily raised the ambient temperature, allowing any absorbent items to dry out.

And the text on the display of the Planet Assessment Computer was now visible. It read:

ANDROMEDA GALAXY: UNIDENTIFIED PLANET
OXYGEN/NITROGEN BASED ATMOSPHERE
TEMPERATURE MODERATE
H2O DETECTED
WILL SUPPORT CARBON BASED LIFE

And now, eighty-seven years after its launch, with a habitable planet identified, the fungus gone, and the interior of the ship in pristine condition, the *Prometheus* fired its retro rockets to slow itself down. In about three days, it would gently land on a beautiful beach in a bountiful land.

This event would fulfill the vision of two people: a man named Ryan Van Lank, who, almost a century ago, dreamed he could reach a place he called Xanadu, Shangri-La, the Garden of Eden. And a young woman named Sandra Hapgood, who discovered a way to digitize people but, more importantly, developed a process to bring them back to human form, to God's image.

And as the ship zeroed in on this New World, Recombinant Labs Three and Four came to life. In both cylinders, multi-colored streams of water, minerals, and proteins began to swirl, ready to re-instantiate two human beings.

In the Strand Data Room, the computer that was controlling the Lab cylinders displayed two, green-rimmed images on its monitor. One was a photo of a young blonde girl. The text beneath the photo identified her as EVELYN HIMMEL.

The other image was not a photo, but a generic icon of a baby boy. His name was ADAM HAPGOOD.

And as the *Prometheus* veered to starboard, to bring it in line with the bright, blue planet, it left in its wake the vastness of space, a display of the cosmos in all its beauty:

Countless stars;

Boundless distance;

Infinite time.

www.ingramcontent.com/pod-product-compliance
Lightning Source LLC
Chambersburg PA
CBHW070855250626
47159CB00003B/1070